Just who did he think he was?

What did he think he could possibly have to say to her that would justify the kind of arrogance he was displaying? Demanding to see *her*.

He was still smiling as Jane marched into the cubicle. She didn't bother pulling the curtain.

'Hi.' He stood up, adjusting the burden he held carefully.

Jane said nothing. He had three seconds, max, to say something that might get him off the hook. And if he didn't manage that, he was going to feel the brunt of every frustration and extra bit of pressure she'd been under for the entire week. Jane was drawing in a long, slow breath. Ready to let loose.

'Meet Sophie,' the stranger said, holding out the bundle in his arms. 'Your daughter.'

Alison Roberts lives in Christchurch, New Zealand. She began her working career as a primary school teacher, but now juggles available working hours between writing and active duty as an ambulance officer. Throwing in a large dose of parenting, housework, gardening and pet-minding keeps life busy, and teenage daughter Becky is responsible for an increasing number of days spent on equestrian pursuits. Finding time for everything can be a challenge, but the rewards make the effort more than worthwhile.

Recent titles by the same author:

HOT-SHOT SURGEON, CINDERELLA BRIDE
THE ITALIAN SURGEON'S CHRISTMAS
    MIRACLE
ONE NIGHT WITH HER BOSS
MARRYING THE MILLIONAIRE DOCTOR*

Crocodile Creek

HER BABY
OUT OF THE BLUE

BY
ALISON ROBERTS

First published in Great Britain 2009
Large Print edition 2010
Harlequin Mills & Boon Limited,
Eton House, 18-24 Paradise Road,
Richmond, Surrey TW9 1SR

© Alison Roberts 2009

ISBN: 978 0 263 21085 9

Harlequin Mills & Boon policy is to use papers that are
natural, renewable and recyclable products and made
from wood grown in sustainable forests. The logging and
manufacturing process conform to the legal environmental
regulations of the country of origin.

Printed and bound in Great Britain
by CPI Antony Rowe, Chippenham, Wiltshire

HER BABY
OUT OF THE BLUE

CHAPTER ONE

'*YES*! I think we've found her.'

Dylan McKenzie straightened in his chair, his heart beating a little faster as he recognised the figure. The bundle in his arms squirmed at the soft sound of his voice but Sophie didn't wake, bless her. She had been as patient as he'd had to be, waiting for this Jane Walters to answer her pager.

Not that it had been a problem. You couldn't just walk into an emergency department and demand that a surgeon be summoned from Theatre. Even for something as important as this.

He couldn't cross the busy department and introduce himself either. He had to leave that up to the cute triage nurse, Mandy, who had been kind enough to let him sit in this empty cubicle while he waited. He tried to catch Mandy's attention now, to alert her to the brisk arrival of the woman in surgical scrubs who had entered through the double doors leading further into this big city hospital.

But Mandy was bending over an ambulance stretcher, talking to an elderly woman.

'Are you having any chest pain now?'

'Just a little, dear. Nothing to bother about. It's much better than it was.'

'She's had five milligrams of morphine,' a paramedic told Mandy.

Dylan took a second look at the latest arrival to the department. *Was* it her? She looked to be in her mid-thirties and a wisp or two of dark blonde hair had escaped the disposable hat she was wearing, but she didn't look exactly like the photograph he had currently tucked away in his pocket next to his passport and a crumpled boarding pass.

The baggy scrub suit was a good disguise but it was more the way this woman held herself that prompted the doubt. Dylan had the feeling that when she got changed, her civvies would be very smart. A slim-fitting black skirt, perhaps, with a tailored jacket to match. And boots. Definitely boots. Black, with spiky heels.

'Let's get her into Resus 2. I think it's free.' Mandy turned to check the availability of a space with cardiac monitoring facilities and must have seen the surgeon, because her head swung around to look for Dylan and her quick smile and nod suggested she would be able to attend to his request as soon as this patient was sorted.

So it *was* her. Even though the woman in his photograph was wearing jeans rolled up to her knees with her toes covered by soft white sand and had hair that kind of flowed to rest on her shoulders and—maybe the biggest difference— she was smiling.

This woman, now being intercepted by Mandy, was not smiling.

'Dr Walters?' Mandy's call sounded faintly through the hum of the activity around them.

It was inconvenient the way many female surgeons preferred to be called 'Doctor'. Now that Dylan had confirmation of her identity, it would have been useful to add her marital status to the information he was gathering. Was there a husband in the picture? Children?

He hoped not. Why hadn't he thought to ask Josh about details like that? Because it hadn't seemed important at the time, that's why. Dylan's breath escaped in a sigh as he shut away memories fresh enough to have the potential to derail him.

It was impossible to hear what Mandy was saying now but it was obvious she was informing Dr Walters that he had asked to see her. Maybe that he'd been waiting a long time. He felt the intensity of the glance that came his way and saw how her eyes widened just enough to advertise surprise.

OK, it had been a slight exaggeration to say he knew her. That he was a friend. But they would hardly have paged her otherwise, would they?

She was frowning now. Quite possibly displeased at having her busy schedule interrupted by something this random. She would be trying to make sense of it. Wondering whether she had, in fact, ever met him before.

Dylan could sense imminent dismissal. He

couldn't let that happen so he did something that almost always achieved the desired result.

He smiled at her.

Who the hell was he?

Attractive young men did not generally sit in the ED and smile at her as if…as if just *seeing* her was enough to make him happy. His curly hair was far too long and he was wearing a black T-shirt beneath a leather jacket that looked old and very soft. His blue jeans were so faded the knees were white and did those scuffed-looking toes belong to *cowboy* boots? He probably had a gold ring in one of his ears.

While he didn't look at all put out to be holding a baby, Jane had the distinct impression he would look even more at home holding a guitar. Sitting by a camp fire, maybe, with a gypsy caravan in the background. Certainly not the type of person she ever encountered in her limited social circle.

'He said he knew me?'

Mandy nodded. 'He's got a baby with him. Her name's Sophie and she's about four weeks old. Such a cutie—'

'Is the baby sick?' Was he a parent of a recent patient? No. The last neonate she'd been called to see had been a couple of weeks ago. A newborn boy with a cleft palate serious enough to make feeding an issue.

'No.' Mandy shook her head this time. 'At least, I don't think so. All he said was that he really needed to see you.'

'And he's been waiting how long?'

'A couple of hours? Maybe more. I rang Theatre as soon as he arrived but you were just starting a case.'

A long, complicated case. The end of a back-to-back load that had left Jane with aching muscles and a strong desire for a hot shower and a break she couldn't afford to take. A ward round that would probably keep her in this building until 8 p.m. was waiting. She should have sent her registrar to deal with this. Irritation at precious time being wasted surfaced.

'And you've let him take up a cubicle space in Emergency for that whole time?'

Mandy flushed. 'He was so… I…'

Jane could feel her lips pressing themselves

into a thin line. He'd smiled at her, hadn't he? Of course Mandy would have melted under a smile like that, especially when it belonged to a tall, more than slightly disreputable-looking young man with a mop of unruly black curls and a cute baby in his arms.

Why was he here with a baby?

Jane made the mistake of taking a second glance. She didn't know him and she certainly wasn't a friend. For whatever reason, this man had lied in order to see her and now he was sitting there, taking up valuable space in a busy department with the most *unrepentant* smile she had ever seen. Charming, maybe. Irresponsible, definitely.

'Oh, for heaven's sake,' she muttered. 'Fine. I'll talk to him.'

She'd talk to him all right. He was going to get an earful of just how busy clinicians in this hospital were. How short-staffed nurses were. How unhelpful it was to take up space that could be used by someone who genuinely needed it.

Just who did he think he was?

What did he think he could possibly have to

say to her that would justify the kind of arrogance he was displaying? Demanding to see *her*.

He was still smiling as Jane marched into the cubicle. She didn't bother pulling the curtain.

'Hi.' He stood up, adjusting the burden he held carefully.

Jane said nothing. He had three seconds, max, to say something that might get him off the hook. And if he didn't manage that, he was going to feel the brunt of every frustration and extra bit of pressure she'd been under for the entire week. Jane was drawing in a long, slow breath. Ready to let loose.

'Meet Sophie,' the stranger said, holding out the bundle in his arms. 'Your daughter.'

CHAPTER TWO

'*EXCUSE* me?'

Jane whisked the curtain shut behind her. Mandy was watching but hopefully she had been too far away to hear that extraordinary introduction. She turned back to what now felt like a small space. There was a narrow bed and a single chair beside it. A baby's car seat with a handle was on the floor beside the chair and it had a bag inside it with what looked like a nappy poking through the zip. The rest of the space was taken up by a very large man holding a very small baby. Jane glared at the man.

'*What* did you just say?'

'This is Sophie,' the stranger repeated patiently. At least he spoke more quietly this time.

Maybe Jane's horrified whisper had made him realise his mistake.

'Sophie McKenzie,' he continued. 'I'm Dylan McKenzie. My older brother was Josh and he was married to—'

'Izzy,' Jane finished for him, her tone hollow.

A tiny silence fell in which the name seemed to hang in the air despite the busy sounds from outside the curtain. A patient groaning in the next cubicle. A child shrieking a little further away. The rattle of an IV trolley going past and the general paging system requesting a doctor in Resus 1 immediately.

Izzy. Jane's best friend. At times wild, always passionate, the life of any party. The person she'd loved enough to go way further than an extra mile for. Her fellow student, flatmate…the sister she'd never had.

Dylan was watching her. He had dark blue eyes, Jane thought irrelevantly. And black hair and fair skin. Irish colouring but his accent was Scottish. Josh had been Scottish, too. Working abroad as a registrar when he'd met Izzy and they'd fallen madly in love.

'The love of my life,' Izzy had said more than once. 'My soulmate. This is death-till-we-part stuff, Janey.'

The expression in those dark blue eyes looked horribly like…sympathy.

'Where is she?' Jane's voice came out sounding strange. A kind of soft croak. She knew, dammit. *This* was why the emails had stopped and the phone messages hadn't been returned. She still had to ask. 'What's happened?'

'I'm so sorry.' The accent became stronger as his voice dropped. 'But Izzy died. A month ago now.'

Jane gasped. A moment ago all those sounds around them had been quite intelligible. A familiar cacophony Jane was so used to she could just pick what she needed to hear from it. Now those sounds became a buzz that pressed in on her ears like waves. Rushing in and then receding. She had no idea she was swaying on her feet until she felt her arm gripped firmly.

'Sit down,' came the command.

Jane sat on the uncomfortable wooden chair beside the bed.

'Put your head down,' the voice continued. 'Should I call someone for you?'

'N-no!' The buzzing receded enough for Jane's mind to grasp something solid. The knowledge that this was very personal.

Private business.

She put a hand over her eyes. Took a breath and then another. Then she dropped the hand and looked up.

'I'm sorry,' Dylan said again.

He meant it. If he hadn't had a baby in his arms, Jane was sure he would have hugged her. Not that she would have welcomed a hug from a complete stranger, of course. She stared at him for a moment longer. Why did she have the ridiculous disappointment that he *was* holding that baby, then?

'I think,' she said slowly, 'that you'd better tell me everything.'

'That's why I'm here.'

Jane gave her head a tiny shake. 'No, not here.'

He looked over his shoulder, as though he could see through the curtain to the noisy, crowded area it screened. 'Fair enough. Where?'

'My office, I suppose.'

'Now?'

'Do you have the time?'

A hint of a smile pulled at the corners of his mouth and for a moment his whole face lightened. 'I've travelled all the way from Edinburgh for this, hen. I've all the time in the world.' He raised a black eyebrow. 'More to the point, have *you* the time?'

'I'll find it.' Jane stood up carefully, trying to push back the devastating news she had just received. Not Izzy. Oh, *God*! She couldn't deal with it just yet. Thank goodness her training and her job enabled the kind of self-control she needed rather badly right now. 'Come with me.'

Mandy was still watching from behind the triage desk. She stared at Jane.

'Are you all right, Dr Walters?'

'Of course.'

'Is there anything…?'

Mandy was clearly disconcerted. Did she look that awful? Jane pulled off the disposable hat and ran her hand over her head to check that her hair was still mostly confined in the neat braid. The nurse's gaze slid past her to Dylan, who had the baby on one arm and the car seat and bag in his other hand. 'Your backpack…?'

'Could I leave it with you just for now?'

Mandy was getting one of those killer smiles. Jane could tell by the way the nurse breathed out in what looked like a soft sigh. 'Sure. It's out of the way in the ambulance bay locker.'

'There is something you could do, Mandy.' Jane was pleased to hear her voice sounding almost normal. 'Page my registrar and tell him to start the ward round without me. I'll catch up with the post-ops later. For anything urgent, I can be paged.'

It was quite a walk to Dr Walters's office.

A silent walk apart from the occasional greeting directed at the woman half a step ahead of Dylan.

'Dr Walters.'

'Jane! How are you?'

She acknowledged the greetings but her step never wavered. Her back was straight, her gaze fixed on a point well ahead of them and her stride determined enough for Dylan's long legs to move at a comfortable pace.

He stole more than one sideways glance. This Jane Walters was considerably more pale than she had been when he had first set eyes on her, but was that the only indication she might be upset? Were her features always this set?

Ice Queen sprang to mind.

Except it didn't quite fit.

Dylan had met his sister-in-law some time ago now. Last Christmas, when the couple had arrived back in Scotland. Izzy had been a delight. So vibrant. So full of life and laughter, and she had talked about Jane all the time. Her very best friend that she missed terribly. The person who was going to be so excited when—*if* the miracle really happened.

The miracle *had* happened.

But right now Dylan found he couldn't imagine Jane Walters getting excited about anything. Pleased, perhaps. Satisfied, certainly. The notion that excitement could dent the aura of control— power, even—that emanated from this slim figure he was following was quite bizarre.

She was important here, that was obvious. She might be oblivious to the quick glances and smiles that advertised respect but Dylan wasn't. He knew the kind of hierarchy that existed in hospitals only too well and he knew he was walking with royalty.

And if he hadn't picked it up on the journey, he couldn't have missed the information from the office he was ushered into. By the standards of most hospitals, it was palatial. With a view to the beautiful city park that bordered the hospital grounds. A glimpse of the river even.

There was a wall completely covered with framed diplomas and postgraduate degrees and floor-to-ceiling shelving with meticulously filed stacks of medical journals and a wealth of reference books. The blotter on the surface of the large desk was unsullied by any doodling and the chair was tidily pushed in. Jane didn't go to that side of her desk, however. She stopped beside one of the two comfortable armchairs that flanked a coffee table.

'Have a seat,' she directed. 'Um…does the baby need anything?'

'Her name's Sophie.' Dylan's smile felt forced. God, he was tired. 'And no, she's fine for the moment. I fed and changed her while we were waiting in Emergency.'

'Right.' Jane sat on the edge of the other chair, which made her look uncomfortable. Her hands were curled into loose fists and the skin around her nose and mouth was pale enough to be of concern.

She looked terrible, Dylan decided. He was studying her face as she raised her gaze and then he couldn't look away. She had an unusual eye colour. Green? Brown? He couldn't tell because the pupils were large. She looked… grief-stricken.

'What happened?' A tiny catch in her voice added to his impression. 'Was it a complication of childbirth?'

'No. That all went perfectly. They were taking Sophie home from the hospital a few days after the birth and there was an accident on the M1. Izzy was killed instantly. Josh…broke his neck. He survived in the spinal unit for three weeks but died of respiratory complications.' Dylan had to pause for a moment. 'Actually,' he added softly, 'I think he died of a broken heart.'

'And the…? And Sophie? She was in the car?'

'She was in her new state-of-the-art car seat.' Dylan tilted his head to where he'd left the items he had carried with him on the floor beside his chair. 'She's fine.' He looked down at the tiny face he could see in the folds of soft blanket. His arms tightened a little and something huge squeezed his heart. 'Better than fine,' he added. 'She's perfect.'

Jane wasn't looking at Sophie. She was staring at her hands, now tightly clasped in her lap.

'I knew something was wrong. Izzy had been hinting at a surprise and, at first, I thought they were planning a visit back to Christchurch. I've been half expecting to open my door and find them there, laughing at me. It's never been this long without an email or phone call. I've rung so many times.'

'I got the message you left last week.'

'Why didn't you contact me, then? Why didn't someone call me as soon as it had happened?' There was anger in her voice now. 'Josh knew how close Izzy and I were. He must have known I'd want to be there for…for her funeral. I was the only real family Izzy had.'

'Izzy was a McKenzie,' Dylan said steadily. 'My sister-in-law. My brother's wife. My father's daughter-in-law. The only daughter he ever had. *We* were her family. And we all loved her.'

Eyebrows a shade or two darker than the rich golden brown of Jane's hair were lowered into a scowl. She didn't like that.

'Josh was too ill that first week,' Dylan continued. 'On a ventilator in the intensive care unit. My father was distraught. I had to make all the arrangements. All the decisions.'

'You had no right to exclude me.'

'I'm sorry.' And he was. He hadn't bargained on this. The grief he could feel. Jane had been just a name. An entity a world away from the tragedy he'd been dealing with. He hated that he was causing her so much pain. 'There was someone else who had to take priority in all the decisions I made.' He glanced down again and his voice softened. 'This wee lassie.'

Dylan looked up and waited until Jane met his gaze. 'Your daughter,' he added.

'*No!*' Jane shot up as though her chair had

scorched her. 'You've made a mistake. There's no way this child is mine.'

Dylan had to look up a lot further this time but he remained sitting. He had to try and stay calm. This was a shock for her, he reminded himself. She needed time. She needed to see Sophie. Really look at her. Touch her. And then she would feel the way he did. That nothing mattered except for what was going to be best for this precious baby.

Was she distracting herself from grief for her friend by launching herself into denial? She was certainly focused. Controlled. Attributes she needed, no doubt, in order to perform her job. He needed to be controlled himself. Stick to the facts if he could and not let emotion take over.

'My understanding is that you donated the eggs that Josh and Izzy used for their IVF treatments.'

Jane's breath came out in an exasperated huff. 'Yes…but that was more than two years ago. The treatments failed. Both of them. Izzy was too upset to think about doing it again. That's why they decided to go back to Scotland. To start a new life.' Jane had turned and was pacing towards the bookshelves. She whirled back to face Dylan. 'I was there. We were all upset that it hadn't worked but I didn't offer to provide any more eggs and Izzy didn't ask.'

'There was a final embryo. When they were tying up loose ends before they left the country, they contacted the fertility clinic and were told about it and asked to make a decision about whether to keep it or not. I don't know why it had been kept and not used in the earlier attempts. Josh said something about its viability being in question.'

'There were only four viable embryos. Two got implanted with each attempt. Both attempts failed. That was the end of it.'

Dylan nodded. He could understand why Jane was so adamant. 'That's what they thought as well but apparently there was the extra one. The odds of the implantation being successful were minimal but they decided to use it so they wouldn't be left wondering.'

'No.' Jane shook her head decisively. 'Izzy would have told me.'

'She didn't think it would work. She didn't want to raise anyone's hopes, especially her own. She thought if she and Josh were the only people to know, it would be easier to deal with another failure. She had the implantation procedure and that was it as far as they were concerned. They'd tried their best and it was time to put it all behind them and start a new life.'

A flash of pain appeared to mix with the anger and sheer disbelief on Jane's face. Was she feeling shut out? Distressed that her best friend could have kept such a secret from her?

'She would have told me when she knew she was pregnant.'

'She couldn't believe it to start with. Didn't she lose a baby the first time? At about eight or nine weeks?'

Jane gave a single nod.

'They waited until they thought it was safe and then they waited because they wanted to surprise you.'

'How do *you* know so much about this?'

Yes. There was jealousy there. And pain. A lot of pain. Not really an ice queen, then, despite her attempts to appear perfectly in control.

'Josh was my brother,' Dylan said gently. 'He was a few years older than me but we were very close. We lost Mum when we were quite young and there was just the three of us. Josh was like another parent as well as my best mate.'

He drew in a ragged breath. No more tears, he told himself. Not here. Not in front of her. *Please*.

'He came out of Intensive Care and I had two weeks sitting beside his bed in the spinal unit. Sleeping beside it. Dad and I took turns but it was too hard on my father so I stayed virtually the whole time.'

He had to sniff. To clear his throat. 'There was nothing to do apart from hold his hand and talk. To let him meet his daughter. To let him grieve for Izzy—the love of his life. And to grieve for the future he was never going to have.'

The pain in his voice was palpable.

Jane had never had a sibling but she'd had her chosen sister, Izzy. How would it have been to have been sitting with *her* for weeks if her beloved Josh was gone? With them both knowing that even if she survived she would be unable to look after the baby she had longed for so desperately?

It was unimaginable. Jane's heart went out to this man sitting here with the baby. Swallowing the painful lump in her throat, Jane moved slowly back to the empty chair and sat down.

'I'm sorry.' She closed her eyes as she sighed. Words could be so inadequate at times. 'It must have been terrible for you. Josh was…he was a lovely guy.'

'You knew him?' The tone of surprise was squashed. 'Of course you did, with you and Izzy being so close.'

'We lived together. Josh moved in with us within a few days of meeting Izzy.' Jane found a smile. 'It really was a case of love at first sight.'

'I would have come for the wedding if I'd been invited.'

He sounded…jealous? Jane had shared a special moment of his brother's life that he'd been excluded from. She couldn't feel sorry for him, surely, after what *she'd* been excluded from.

Maybe she could.

'It was a spur-of-the-moment thing. A celebrant, a beach and a couple of surfers for witnesses. Izzy and Josh said it was the commitment to each other that mattered, not putting on a show for anyone else.' Another smile tugged at her mouth even as something sad and raw twisted inside her. 'We all wore jeans and we went paddling afterwards.'

'In jeans? On a beach?' Dylan shifted the baby in his arms and fished in the pocket of his well-worn leather jacket. A slightly crumpled photograph was produced. 'Was that when this picture was taken?'

'Yes.' Jane had to press her lips together. She didn't want to cry in front of a stranger. She needed to wind this interview up and have a little time to herself, hopefully, before her pager summoned her. 'That…that was my official bridesmaid portrait.'

Dylan shook his head. 'Why did it have to be so rushed? I would have come.'

'It was kind of a celebration, I guess.'

'Of what?'

Jane sighed. 'Maybe resolution would be a better word. It had been a rather intense few weeks. Josh had proposed but Izzy refused to marry him and it was tearing her to pieces. Tearing us all to pieces.'

Dylan's eyebrows rose. 'I thought it was love at first sight? Why did she refuse?'

At least there was something Jane knew more about than Izzy's brother-in-law.

'She knew she couldn't have babies and there was nothing Josh could say that would convince her it didn't matter. Izzy could get very passionate about things. She had got it into her head that the only way she could show Josh how much she loved him was to have his baby.'

'And why couldn't she?'

'Early menopause. Hit her at twenty-nine. Way before she met Josh. There was no warning, either, so she couldn't try and harvest her own eggs and store them.'

'So you stepped in and offered yours?'

'Not exactly.' He made it sound as if it had been a casual thing. An easy solution. 'As I said, it was…intense.' Fraught, more like. Izzy had made it seem that futures and friendships were on the line. 'Izzy knew I was never going to have my own children. I—'

'Why?' The interruption was puzzled. 'How did you know that for sure?'

'Because I made a choice to have a career that doesn't leave time to raise children, that's why.' Jane's tone hardened. 'Because my parents had full-on careers and I know what it's like to be raised by parents who don't have the time.' Not that her upbringing was any of his business. 'Yes, I got persuaded to help Izzy but, if I'm honest, I had doubts about it. There was an element of relief when it didn't work.'

'But it did work.'

As if to support the quiet statement, the baby in his arms stirred and squeaked.

I'm here, the noise said. *I'm real.*

'I have her birth certificate if you'd like to see it.'

A cold prickle ran down Jane's spine. 'And that's relevant because…?'

'Because it has your name on it. As her mother.'

'I'm *not* her mother!'

'Biologically, you are. It was Josh who

thought it was the best plan. We got legal advice and medical records as supportive evidence. You signed a consent to have your identity available.'

'Only in case of a family medical history being needed. Or…a bone-marrow transplant or something.' Jane stood up again. She needed to move. 'This is ridiculous. I did not choose to have a child.'

Sophie squeaked more loudly. A grizzle that threatened to turn into a cry. Did she sense the rejection?

'There's lots of mothers out there who didn't exactly choose to have a child.' The outrageous calm of Dylan's voice showed he had absolutely no understanding of the implications of this situation. 'They still bond with them when they arrive. They bring them up and they make good mothers.'

'I have no intention of bonding with this baby.' Oh, Lord, that sounded callous but it was the truth. 'And I'm not about to have motherhood forced on me.'

Jane was pacing again. Towards her desk. Her nice tidy desk—as organised and precise as her life. There was the gold clock, the box of pens, a pad of sticky notes, another box with her business cards.

'Here.' Jane picked up one of the cards and marched back to present it to Dylan. 'Here are my contact details. Call me tomorrow when I've had time to contact my solicitors. We'll sort something out. A way I can contribute to this child's welfare.'

'That's big of you.' Dylan took the card and stuffed it into his pocket. He stood up, seemingly oblivious to the steady wail Sophie was now emitting. 'But wee Sophie needs a bit more than money.'

'It's the best I can offer.'

'I don't agree.'

'Look.' The noise the baby was making was filling Jane's head and making it impossible to think clearly. She had to escape. Find time to think about this. 'She's got you. You're her uncle and you obviously care about her. I'll help however I can but—'

Along with the strident sound of a distressed baby came the insistent beeping of Jane's pager.

She was needed. Where she belonged. In the paediatric intensive care unit or the ward or an operating theatre. She had to escape and step back into her real life.

Away from this nightmare.

Jane turned, ready to pick up the telephone on her desk and find out where she was needed.

'Oi!'

Jane's jaw dropped. Her astonishment at such an inappropriate command was enough to actually make her turn back.

'You made a choice,' Dylan said, his voice low and dangerous. 'You made it possible for this baby to come into the world. You have to take responsibility for that choice.'

'But I *told* you. I—'

'No.' He was furious now, the word was ground out from a clenched jaw. 'I won't have it. Sophie deserves better than this. *Sophie*,' he repeated, holding out the shrieking bundle. '*Your* daughter.'

She had no idea how it happened. It was all too fast and noisy and totally unexpected. There she was, facing an angry man and a baby making a sound that would scramble anyone's brains, and a heartbeat later—here she was…

Holding that baby and watching incredulously as the man stormed out of her office.

CHAPTER THREE

How could he have done that?

Walked out and left her—literally—holding the baby?

An incredulous huff left Jane's lungs as she scanned the now deserted corridor outside her office.

'Shh!' She jiggled the baby but, if anything, the decibel level increased.

Jane stepped back into her office and shut the door with her foot. Perhaps it was lucky the corridor *was* deserted. What would her colleagues think of this?

Jane Walters—dedicated paediatric surgeon who was letting nothing interfere with her meteoric rise through the consultant ranks. An accidental mother? Without ever having had sex with the baby's father or having been pregnant?

There would be an endless stream of jokes about immaculate conceptions and stress-free pregnancies. People would be sniggering at her instead of giving her the respect she had worked so hard to earn.

With an inward groan, Jane recognised the kind of single-minded focus she had given her career taking over yet again. This was rather bigger than being labelled a nerd because she wanted to study instead of partying, however. She was turning the spotlight on herself and her career instead of what actually mattered in this moment of time.

Izzy…

No. She couldn't go there and imagine a world without the person she loved the most. Falling to pieces here and now wasn't going to help anyone, and if it became known it might do more damage to her credibility than producing an unexpected baby.

Izzy's baby.

One that she had wanted desperately enough

to beg *her* for help. What if Izzy could see her now? It was too easy to imagine her friend's passionate expression. To feel the bond that had made them so close.

Please, Izzy would say. *You have to help me here, Janey. You're the only person who can.*

'Shh!' Jane tried to push away the echo of Izzy's voice. She looked down at the tiny, screwed-up face amongst the folds of fuzzy blanket. 'Goodness, you're red!' she exclaimed. 'Is there something wrong with you, baby?'

She could deal with that. Jane sat on the edge of the chair and leaned forward to lay the bundle down carefully on the floor. She peeled back the blanket.

Izzy's baby, she reminded herself as she looked at tiny starfish hands and a miniature body in a soft, stretchy, pink suit.

'Maybe you're too hot.'

It certainly felt hot. And damp. And the smell was a lot less than pleasant. Jane found herself automatically looking up, half expecting a nurse or parent to step in and deal with this.

Jane diagnosed things. She saw babies when

they were clean and awake. Often when they were crying like this, in fact. She saw them later, when they were sedated and quiet and again when they were recuperating and, of course, the time she almost loved the most—when they were completely asleep.

Anaesthetised.

A time when she could use her not inconsiderable powers of concentration and learned skills to fix whatever was wrong and make life a whole lot better for them.

Jane Walters did not change dirty nappies. Or feed babies. She cuddled them sometimes. Once she got to know them—inside and out—they were a part of her professional life and she cared passionately about those children. So much so that she'd never once regretted her decision not to have children of her own. She didn't have the time or need for them. Being able to go home and have a complete break was what enabled her to give everything she had—and more sometimes—to her patients.

This baby had sprung from her personal life, not her professional one. Jane didn't cuddle babies like this. Not when they needed the kind of attention a nurse could deliver much more effectively. Not when they needed their mothers.

Oh…. *God*!

Jane stared down at the miserable scrap of humanity on her floor.

Was it really possible she *was* the closest thing to a real mother this child would ever have? No. Being a mother had far more to do with what happened after the biological chemistry took place. She wasn't a mother. She couldn't even begin to feel like a mother. She didn't *want* to!

The ringing of her desk phone took a while to penetrate both the noise of Sophie crying and Jane's stunned thought processes. By leaning back in her chair she could reach the phone on the corner of her desk.

'Dr Walters?'

It was her registrar. 'Mike. How's it going?'

'Did you get my pager message?'

Good grief. Jane had completely forgotten her pager had even sounded. Her life was in chaos.

'Hang on.' She unclipped it from the elastic band of her scrub suit pants. 'You're in ICU?'

'Yes. Where are you?'

'Um…' There was no way he wouldn't be able to hear the background noise. 'I had to go down to Emergency.'

'Sounds like you've got an unhappy customer.'

'Yes.' The baby was still howling but it was a tired sound now, with an occasional, miserable hiccup. Jane's gaze slid towards the car seat Dylan McKenzie had also left behind. To the bag with the visible nappy. Was there a bottle in there as well? Formula?

'A neonate?' Mike sounded interested at the prospect of a new patient.

'Yes.' Jane needed to change the subject. To find out what Mike wanted and then get off the phone so she could try and think of how to cope. 'What's happening with William? He looked stable when I saw him in Recovery.'

'He's tachycardic. Blood pressure's dropped a bit.'

'Any abdominal signs? What's happening with drainage?'

'I can't see any indication of bleeding. Drainage is minimal. There's no distension.'

'Urine output?'

'Also minimal.'

'Oxygen saturation?'

'Good. Ninety-eight per cent.'

'Increase the rate of IV fluids and see if you can get his BP stable. I'll be up as soon as I can. I just need a few minutes to sort this…'

What—this baby? The situation? The feeling like she'd been sideswiped from her chosen path through life and was falling into a huge crevasse?

Mike didn't wait for an explanation. As always, he was eager to impress. 'I'll be here. I've finished on the ward for now. Everything's looking good.'

'Fine. I'll pop in there later.'

Jane ended the call. The ward wasn't far away. The charge nurse, Margaret, was experienced and unflappable. Just the person Jane needed right now.

My friend's in trouble, she practised silently as she wrapped Sophie back in her blanket and took the bag from the car seat. *A family emergency. I've got to look after this baby for a little while and I really need some assistance. Just until I've seen all my patients.*

And possibly taken one back to Theatre, but even so it shouldn't be for more than an hour or two. Jane eased the safety strap over the lumpy bundle and secured Sophie into the carry seat.

And what then?

Jane carried the seat in one hand and the bag in the other, leaving her office and heading towards the paediatric wards. What if Izzy's brother-in-law didn't come back and take over the care of this infant?

She couldn't very well leave it in the hospital overnight. Questions would be asked. Social Services might be contacted. The truth would emerge.

At least it was Friday. At worst, if she had to take the baby home, all she had to deal with workwise tomorrow was a morning ward round. Then she would have until Monday morning to get this mess sorted out.

And she would get it sorted out.

There was simply no alternative.

Nine p.m.

Dylan McKenzie returned the smiles from a

group of young girls who teetered on their high heels as they passed the park bench he was sitting on. The ones who weren't flat out texting absent friends on their mobile phones turned their heads for another look.

'Come with us,' one of them called cheekily. 'It's Friday night. Time to party!'

Dylan shook his head, his smile fading. 'I've got a date,' he responded. 'But you have fun. And take care,' he added.

They were far too young to be heading for a night on the town in their skimpy tops and tight jeans. No more than fifteen or sixteen, surely? Did their parents know where they were and what they were up to?

Would Sophie be off doing things like this when she should still be safely under adult supervision?

Dylan sighed. Funny how one's view of the world changed so dramatically when one became a parent.

Or an almost parent.

He sighed again. More than twenty-four hours of travelling to get from Edinburgh, Scotland, to

Christchurch, New Zealand, were taking their toll. He'd never felt this tired.

Or this despondent.

Okay, he'd hardly expected Jane Walters to fall over herself in delighted surprise at being presented with her baby but she'd been so obviously uninterested. Appalled, in fact.

She didn't want Sophie.

She'd offered him *money* to try and make the problem go away.

Not many things made Dylan really furious. He prided himself on being able to see both sides of any conflict and being able to retain dignity, if not a sense of humour, in dealing with adverse circumstances, but that had made him angry.

So angry that walking out had seemed the only way to make his point. That Dr Walters had to shoulder at least some of the responsibility. And he'd been worried sick ever since.

What was happening? She might have left Sophie in the care of someone else. It wouldn't be impossible for someone in her position to engage the help of the paediatric ward staff, for instance, and knowing that had been why Dylan hadn't immediately turned round and gone back after his dramatic exit.

But she might have called the police. They might be hunting for him right now, with a warrant for his arrest for having abandoned a helpless baby. If so, he'd be easy enough to find, sitting here in public view beside the river only a few minutes' walk from the hospital. With a backpack beside him to advertise that he wasn't a local.

He'd been sitting here for a very long time now. Hours. Trying to see a way forward. A future he had never envisioned. It wasn't that he wasn't prepared to turn his world upside down to care for his niece because he was quite willing to do that. So was his father, but they'd both agreed that what Sophie really needed was a mother.

Preferably her own. The woman who was genetically closer to Sophie than either her uncle or her grandfather. It had been worth a try, anyway, but it certainly wasn't looking a likely prospect.

Dylan's legs felt stiff as he finally got up from the bench. According to the business card in his hand and the map now stuffed into the side pocket of his backpack, he was about at the halfway point between the hospital and the address where Jane Walters lived.

She would be home by now. If she had even a spark of responsibility or humanity, she would have taken her baby with her. If she hadn't, that would be that as far as Dylan was concerned. He would find where Sophie was and take her back to the other side of the world.

Why wouldn't she stop crying?

Margaret had said she had just been fed and changed when Jane had collected her from the ward around 8 p.m. Tucked into the car seat, the baby had been happy enough until the short taxi ride to her apartment block had ended. The miserable wailing had started as Jane had slipped the key into the lock of her penthouse door and it hadn't stopped since.

This baby knew it was in the wrong place and with the wrong person and there was nothing Jane could do about that because that's how it was. She paced the distance of her open-plan living, dining and kitchen area. Round and round. Rocking the baby. Talking to her. Trying to reassure both the baby and herself. Trying to unravel the knot of anxiety that could morph into something close to panic as it sat there, like a stone, in her stomach.

She actually felt sick. There had been no time to boil a kettle for a hot drink, let alone think about making any dinner. Jane still hadn't even pulled the drapes that covered the wall of glass overlooking the huge central city park across the road.

'It'll be OK,' she told Sophie. 'He's coming back. You were happy enough with him before, weren't you?'

A lot happier than she was with her biological mother, that was for sure.

'He'll look after you. He loves you.'

He had certainly given the impression that he loved this baby. She had looked so comfortable and safe in those strong, male arms.

'He looks like a very nice man.'

His brother had been at any rate. Jane had never allowed a serious relationship to interfere with her life goals. No, that wasn't entirely true.

The men she'd been attracted to were like herself. Highly intelligent, focused and ambitious, and she was not the type of woman they wanted in their lives. Those men wanted support and admiration, not competition.

Izzy had loved her work and had been smart enough to find it easy, but she had been more than willing to give up any notion of a high-powered job as a consultant to be a wife and mother. She'd been planning to work as a general practitioner. To share a practice and life and parenthood with the man who had captured her heart so completely.

And while Jane couldn't think of anything worse as far as a career went, she'd been envious of that overwhelming kind of love. Like being a mother, it was something she knew she'd chosen not to allow room for in her life.

Sophie was *still* crying. The knot in Jane's stomach was like a cramp now and thoughts of Izzy were crowding in on her. Izzy and Josh. She could imagine how incredulous they would have been to discover the IVF treatment had succeeded. How special it must have been to keep their secret and wait. She could *see* them so clearly. Josh with his hand on an expanding belly and Izzy with her face shining with hope and excitement and love…

And now Jane had tears streaming down her own face as she kept walking, and she was holding Sophie more tightly, her head bent so that the fuzzy duck blanket soaked up her tears. The baby's crying was like an echo of her own grief and Jane hardly heard it until she became aware of the insistent knocking on her door.

Was she disturbing the elderly tenants that lived below? Had they come to see what on earth was going on? To complain?

Jane scrubbed her face with the corner of the blanket and took a deep, shuddering breath, determined to gain control. Her neighbours were going to have to deal with this temporary inconvenience.

Just like she was doing.

The ice queen had been crying!

Dylan gave himself a mental shake. The title was inappropriate.

His anger and anxiety had left in a rush a few

minutes ago when he'd been standing over the
road and had seen Jane walking past her
windows, her head bowed over the bundle she
was holding in her arms.

She'd done the right thing and had taken her
daughter home with her and she was holding
her. Cuddling her. Hearing the sound of the baby
crying had been a surprise. Seeing how wrecked
Jane Walters looked when she opened the door
was disturbing.

She was still very pale and now there were
dark circles under eyes that were reddened and
had drops of moisture clumping the lashes.
Wordlessly, Dylan stepped inside and took
Sophie from her arms.

'Hey, hinny,' he said softly. 'What's the matter?
It's all right. Everything's all right.'

The door closed behind him as he rocked the
baby. From the corner of his eye he saw the way
Jane leaned back against the door and closed
her eyes, folding her arms around herself as
though she still needed something to hold. Dylan
had to fight the urge to use one arm to draw her
close. To…comfort her.

Instead, he pretended complete focus on Sophie and kept his tone neutral.

'Is she hungry?'

'She was fed about an hour ago. And changed.' Jane was straightening up now.

'And have you eaten?'

'N-no.' She sounded surprised that he would ask.

'Neither have I.' Dylan was still rocking Sophie and her cries were fading. 'Have you got enough of something for both of us?'

'I…ah…' Jane was staring at the baby whose eyes—and, mercifully, her mouth—were finally closing. 'How did you do that? What was I doing wrong?'

Dylan smiled. 'Don't take it personally. She knows me, that's all.'

Jane didn't return the smile. Her chin came up and a flash of anger sparked in her eyes. 'So why did you abandon her, then? Leave her with total strangers?'

Dylan's sympathy with the way Jane was looking evaporated. Had she missed the point here entirely? Had he been worried sick for hours for no good reason?

'I wanted you to think about the part you have in this wee lassie's life.'

Jane wasn't looking at Sophie now. She was glaring at Dylan and she had the nerve to look self-righteous.

'I could have called the police. Or Social Services.'

'But you didn't.'

'No. Lucky for you. There are laws about child neglect. *Abandonment.*'

'Why didn't you call them, then?'

Her gaze slid sideways. 'Because I didn't want people knowing about this.'

'Why not?'

'It's private.'

'Maybe you don't want people knowing that you're not prepared to acknowledge your own child?'

'I *am* prepared to acknowledge her! I'm prepared to support her in whatever way I can. I want what's best for her—just like you do. And…' The glance at the sleeping infant was triumphant. 'Being with you is clearly what's best for her.' Jane walked past Dylan. 'Have a seat,' she instructed. 'Make yourself comfortable. I'm make us something to eat and we can talk. Scrambled eggs all right with you?'

'Fine.' But Dylan did not obey the command to be seated. He might be prepared to do anything for wee Sophie but he'd had enough of Dr Walters giving orders. And assuming that she had control and had just made all the decisions that needed to be made. Seething quietly, Dylan walked towards the windows, turned and surveyed what he could see of this luxurious apartment.

Jane was busy in the kitchen area. Opening cupboards and a gleaming stainless-steel refrigerator. A saucepan and a bowl and a tray of eggs were already on the spotless black bench top.

'Very nice,' he said eventually, into a silence that was being broken only by the sound of Jane preparing their meal.

'Thanks. I like it.'

'Close to the hospital.'

'Yes. I take a longer route through the park in the summer and get my exercise that way. It's beautiful.'

'Must be hard—keeping white furniture so clean.'

Jane was cracking eggs into the bowl. 'Not at all. I live alone, have no desire to keep pets and I have a cleaner who comes twice a week.' She turned her head as she reached to pick up a whisk. 'My apartment, like my life, is exactly the way I like it. The way I planned it to be.'

Dylan said nothing. It figured. An important position in a large hospital would leave little time to create a home and this was nothing like a home. It looked like a set for a photo shoot by some house-and-garden publication. The perfect city pad for the young professional. Tasteful, modern, comfortable and…completely without soul.

Had the interior designer chosen the artwork hanging on the walls? Random splashes of colour that were echoes of carefully positioned items like cushions and rugs to try and tone down the sterile white on white of everything else. Here it was well into November but there was no hint of Christmas coming. Did she have a white, artificial tree packed away somewhere? With white icicle lights to hang on it, maybe?

It was all so unsuitable for a baby it was a joke. As funny as trying to imagine Jane changing nappies or playing with a baby in a bath. Blowing bubbles or swimming a plastic duck through the water and making quacking noises.

Except it wasn't funny, was it?

It was incredibly sad.

The eggs were fabulous. Lots of chopped parsley and freshly ground black pepper and thick, toasted wholegrain bread. Jane hadn't realised how hungry she was. Normally, she would have poured herself a nice glass of chilled sauvignon blanc to go with the meal but it didn't seem appropriate tonight. You didn't quaff alcohol when you were looking after a baby, did you?

Except that the responsibility had now been handed back. The relief and release of tension was as good as several glasses of wine could have achieved. Jane took another mouthful of the eggs and savoured it, then glanced up to see Dylan picking up some egg-laden toast with his fingers.

'All right?'

'Wonderful. You can cook.'

'You sound surprised.'

Dylan's grin was charmingly shamefaced. 'I guess it's not a skill I associate with important, busy surgeons.'

'How many important, busy surgeons do you know?'

'Oh, heaps.'

'Oh?'

Curiosity about her unexpected visitor surfaced. He had shed the leather jacket now and looked...larger, somehow. Well-defined muscles on his bare upper arms suggested he was fit. The tan might mean he worked outdoors. The hair was too wild to fit with a white-collar job and... Good grief, she'd been right to suspect an ear piercing. It wasn't a gold ring, though. Just a tiny gold stud.

'So what do you do?' Jane asked.

'I'm a nurse.'

The statement was terse. Cut off by a mouthful of food, but Jane was being watched. Those dark blue eyes were on her face. Waiting for her reaction.

He was a male nurse. She was a female surgeon. Was he expecting some kind of put-down? Jane simply nodded.

'So you and Josh both went into medicine, then. Do you have a specialty area?'

The hesitation was so brief Jane wouldn't have noticed if she hadn't been watching for *his* reaction to her reaction. She saw her words being registered and she saw the wariness leave his eyes and an approving gleam take its place.

And, for some inexplicable reason, she felt like she'd passed a test. Supplied the correct answer. Won a prize, even. A tingle of pleasure made her aware of just how tense and miserable she'd been ever since this man had appeared in her life with his devastating news and his alarming young companion.

'I love kids,' Dylan answered when he'd swallowed. 'I've done a fair bit of time in Theatre but I prefer my patients awake. I've done everything over the years. Nursing's a great job to travel with and I've got the world's itchiest feet. I never stay in one place for more than a few months.'

So she'd been right about more than the ear

piercing. He was a gypsy. Would he cart Sophie from pillar to post with him?

Jane opened her mouth to tell him how unsuitable a life that would be for a young child and then snapped it shut. It wasn't her place to criticise. He loved the baby. She was happy with him. He was a nurse and he loved kids and he was Sophie's uncle. End of story.

Any niggling doubt was erased by looking down to where Sophie was sound asleep in her car seat beside Dylan's chair.

'Is she all right, sleeping in there? Doesn't she need a cot or bassinette or something?'

'She'll be fine. I'll make up a bed with pillows and she can share my bed.' Dylan was scraping up the last of his scrambled eggs. 'When I find one, that is.'

'What do you mean?'

'I came straight to the hospital from the airport. I was going to ask you for a recommendation for accommodation but we didn't really get that far, did we?'

'You mean you haven't got something booked? It's after 10 p.m.! What have you been doing for the last few hours? I thought you'd be getting yourself sorted. With a hotel and a cot and supplies and so on.'

'Did you now?' Dylan's gaze was steady. 'You hoped I'd be riding back in on my white charger to rescue you from any responsibility?'

Jane could feel the heat creeping up from her neck to her cheeks. It was exactly what she'd been hoping.

'Um…how long are you expecting to stay?'

'As long as it takes.'

'As long as *what* takes?' Dismay enveloped Jane. This was actually a very long way from being sorted.

'You need time,' Dylan said calmly. 'A chance to get used to the idea that you're a mother. Your only chance to be one, from what you've said.' He pushed his plate away but he was watching Jane with that intense kind of focus he seemed very good at. 'You never intended having a child and you're not about to change your mind.'

Jane would have confirmed his statement but he didn't give her the chance. He kept talking. Quietly. His voice was compelling.

'If you send us away, we'll go, but you'll probably never see Sophie again. You'll never know what it's like to hold a baby in your arms and know that she's yours. That she's utterly dependent on you and that she's going to love you in a way that no one else can ever love you. Don't be in too much of a hurry to break that connection, Jane. It might very well be the only one you ever have.'

He'd called her Jane. In that soft, lilting tone he'd used throughout that extraordinary short speech.

He'd go away, he said. If she chose. He'd go away and take the baby with him.

She wouldn't have to hear him tell her about the responsibility she should be taking on. She wouldn't have to feel guilty or contemplate the shattering effect this child could have on her life.

She wouldn't have to see him sitting here—so out of place in her perfect apartment—with his big, masculine body and his tousled hair. She wouldn't have to listen to that accent that reminded her of Josh and…and Izzy.

She wouldn't hear him calling her 'Jane' like that. Like he knew her.

Like she mattered.

Jane had to swallow hard. And move. She gathered up the empty plates.

'Fine,' she managed to choke out as she stood up. 'You can stay here tonight.'

CHAPTER FOUR

SOMETHING was different.

Flipping open another set of patient notes that Mike handed her, Jane took a quick glance at her watch. It was 9 a.m. and they were well into their Saturday morning rounds that had started at 8. ICU had been covered and they were on their way around the ward. Not behind or ahead of themselves. Nothing important had been missed. Everything was the same as it always was.

Except it wasn't. Something different, that shouldn't be here at work, was making its presence felt, even though Jane couldn't identify what it was. She tried to push the odd feeling of disquiet away. It was hardly surprising that life seemed slightly out of kilter this morning, given that she'd left a half-naked man and a baby in her apartment.

Well, not really half-naked. Dylan had been wearing those faded blue denim jeans and a singlet when she'd discovered him in her kitchen at 6 a.m. He had been mixing baby formula with one hand, his other arm occupied by holding Sophie, and he was making what had to be an awkward task look effortless.

Jane hadn't heard the baby awaken. The apartment had been peaceful and disconcertingly normal when she'd shut herself in the bathroom for a shower. They must have just emerged from the small spare bedroom when Jane had found them. The baby's fine dark hair had been almost as tousled as her uncle's, but only Dylan had smiled at Jane. Sophie had taken one look and started wailing.

'Coffee,' Jane muttered—as she had done in response to the ear-splittingly loud noise that baby was capable of producing.

'Sorry?' Mike sounded startled. 'You want... um...coffee?'

'No.' Jane gave her head a sharp shake. 'Of

course not. I…' She glanced up from the notes she was holding into the door of the room they were standing outside, her brain finding an escape route with commendable speed. 'Matthew's parents are looking pretty tired, don't you think? They might appreciate a coffee.'

Her registrar gave her a strange look. Jane ignored him and stepped briskly into the room where fifteen-month-old Matthew was standing in his cot, banging a plastic hammer on the top bar. His father was trying to read him a story and his mother, Sarah, was picking up toys that looked as though they had been flung from the cot.

Jane smiled. 'I see Matthew's feeling a lot better.'

Sarah's smile chased much of the weariness from her face. 'Isn't it wonderful? He's almost himself again.'

'Did you get any sleep?'

'Not much.'

'We can let Matthew have a bit more freedom today. He's doing exceptionally well, seeing as his surgery was only three days ago.'

'What about the results?' Matthew's father had discarded the picture book. 'Are they all in now?'

'Most of them. They've confirmed the first results we obtained during the surgery. Matthew's neuroblastoma is definitely Stage 1.'

'That's good, isn't it?' Sarah dropped the toys she was holding into the cot and responded automatically to her son's raised arms and demanding chirps, scooping him up gently to hold him.

'It's the best we could have hoped for,' Jane agreed. 'We've managed to remove the tumour completely and there's very few signs of any microscopic residual disease. Tests on the lymph nodes have all come back negative.'

Tears shone in Sarah's eyes. 'So he's going to be all right?'

'He's low risk.' Jane had to add a note of caution. 'My part in his treatment is over for the moment. The paediatric oncology team will be in to see Matthew and talk to you very soon. They'll be the ones to make any decisions about chemotherapy and any other treatments.'

'So it could come back.' Matthew's father

moved closer to his wife and son. He put his arm around Sarah. Matthew smiled and reached up with a chubby fist.

'Dad dad dad,' he said proudly.

'The five-year survival rate for children with Stage 1 disease is seventy to ninety per cent,' Jane told them, trying to sound upbeat. 'We're going to watch Matthew very carefully but the odds are good. Very good.'

But not good enough, judging by the fear Jane could still see in the eyes of Matthew's parents.

She had seen that fear before. Many times. Jane specialised in dealing with patients like little Matthew who had needed surgery for childhood cancers. She was very good at what she did and she knew that her skills improved the odds for survival. Sometimes even provided a complete cure.

Yes, she was used to seeing that fear. Understanding it and reassuring people as much as possible.

But this time it was different.

Jane could not only see the fear and understand it. She could *feel* it. As if it were her own. As if it were Izzy and Josh standing there, holding

Sophie, and she had just delivered a verdict on odds that didn't sound so great if you turned them around and said that this baby had a ten to thirty per cent chance of *not* surviving.

This was what was different today.

Because her world had tipped and now included a baby she was connected to—whether she liked it or not—Jane was seeing her world through a new perspective.

A dangerous perspective. One that she had deliberately avoided. Yes, she was good at what she did but she intended to get a whole lot better. She couldn't afford distraction or burnout and if she became too emotionally involved with her caseload, that was precisely what could happen.

It wasn't that she couldn't or didn't empathise with her patients and their families, but Jane had to hang on to the clear, scientific perspective that enough distance could provide. She had to think like a doctor, not a parent.

She had always known that if she became a parent it had the potential to cloud her judgement. Colour her decisions. Leach a little more of her strength every time she had a difficult choice to make or a heartbreaking result.

She *couldn't* be a parent.

Sophie seemed to know that, too, because she hated the sight of her, as she had demonstrated so ably again this morning. And that was a good thing. It would make sorting this situation so much easier. It was also good that the rest of this weekend was available to focus on doing exactly that.

Jane popped into the ward office before she left work a little after 11.30 a.m.

'Sally? Thanks again for your help yesterday.'

'My pleasure.' The older nurse manager smiled at Jane. 'What a wee poppet. It was a treat to have a healthy baby to play with for a while.' She reached for the files Jane had put down on the side bench. 'We tend to forget that most of the babies in the world are like her. Our perspective gets a little skewed, working in a place like this.'

'Mmm.' Jane had the disconcerting thought that Sally sensed the way her perception had been challenged that morning.

Had Sally touched on how paediatric doctors who were also parents coped? By being aware of that balance? Did they get to relieve some of the stress engendered by work by appreciating what was normal and healthy?

They still had to be too much in tune with how their patients' parents felt, however, and that had to dilute the kind of focus you needed if you wanted to be exceptional in your field.

The way she intended to be.

Sally was slotting the files into the trolley in alphabetical order. 'Did it get sorted?' she queried. 'The crisis that left you looking after Sophie?'

'We're working on it.' Jane's hesitation was only momentary. Sally had seen it all over the years, hadn't she? She was motherly and wise. 'The baby's actually an orphan.'

'Oh!' Sally's face creased in sympathy. 'The poor wee mite!'

Jane didn't want to go too far down that track and end up feeling too sorry for Sophie. 'Her uncle's looking after her. He loves her.'

'Hmm.' Sally turned back to her filing but cast a sideways glance at Jane. 'I guess he was the one who was waiting to see you in ED yesterday?'

Jane blinked. Hospital grapevines were astonishing information networks. What else did Sally—and everyone else—know?

'Why did he come *here*?' The query was tentative. Sally knew she was stepping over a boundary that could be deemed too personal but her curiosity was clearly getting the better of her.

Jane's secret was still safe, then. The relief was enough to loosen her guard. 'Do you remember Isobel Summers? She was a registrar in ED here until a couple of years ago.'

'The name seems familiar.'

'She was my best friend. She's the…um… she's Sophie's mother. Or was…'

'Oh, no! I'm *so* sorry, Jane. That's awful!'

Jane accepted the sympathy with a tight smile and nod. Sally might be the closest thing to a mother figure in her life but Dr Walters was not going to break down in the ward office.

'Dylan, the…um, Sophie's uncle wanted to tell me the news himself.'

Sally nodded. 'That was kind. I suppose it'll be the grandparents who will raise her. Isobel's family? Is that why he's here?'

'Possibly.'

The option was new and momentarily attractive but, sadly, she had to dismiss it just as quickly. Izzy had long been estranged from her mother, who had been far more involved in her new marriage than her daughter for many years. Why on earth would she be interested in raising a baby that had absolutely no genetic connection to herself?

Suppressing a sigh, Jane turned to leave. 'What I came in for was to say that I'll be out of town for the rest of the weekend. I'll still be available on my mobile, though, and I'm only an hour or so away if I'm needed.'

'You're not on call, are you?'

'No.'

'You shouldn't make yourself so available all the time,' Sally admonished. 'You go and enjoy a bit of peace. Are you going to your mother's place? In Akaroa?'

Jane nodded. 'I haven't been there for a couple of months and the garden will be a mess. I…just need to get away for a day or two.'

She was being forced to get away, more like.

Not that she could dispute how right Dylan had been when he'd pointed out that he and Sophie couldn't possibly stay in her apartment any longer. That it was no place for a baby. She *could* have told him that.

He'd also been right when he'd stated that they needed time to talk about this situation and she even had to agree that a place far enough away from the hospital and the apartment so that she wouldn't be distracted had been a sensible suggestion.

But why, oh, why, had she instantly come up with the idea of using the cottage in Akaroa?

Her private place. Her touchstone.

Because it had been the obvious and ideal solution, that's why. Available. Easy. A quick way to escape the unsettling sound of a baby crying, not to mention the possibly more unsettling sight of Dylan's bare torso.

So the offer had been made and Dylan had approved. It was too late to back out now. It would take too long to find furnished accommodation to rent elsewhere and what was the alternative? Putting them both into a hotel? Hardly a private place to discuss something that had the kind of long-term repercussions this did.

'Of course you do,' Sally was saying kindly. Her expression made it necessary to stamp on any hint of tears once again. 'You've had terrible news. I hope you're going to have some company. Someone that will understand what you're dealing with.'

Jane's smile was wry. 'Oh, yes. I think so.'

'Wow! This is so not the kind of car I would have expected you to drive.'

Jane unlocked the back door of the huge SUV. 'I had it delivered to the hospital this morning. It's on hire.' She flicked what could only be described as a challenging glance in Dylan's direction. 'What sort of car *would* you expect me to be driving?'

Dylan grinned. 'That's easy. Something sleek and sexy. A BMW convertible, probably.'

She went bright red. Was it because she thought Dylan had suggested *she* might be sleek and sexy?

Well, she was, come to think of it. Intimidatingly so, in fact, in the civvies she had probably draped a white coat over for her ward round that morning. That tight-fitting black skirt shaped slim hips and the shirt and waistcoat were trendy but still dignified. The high heels of her black shoes were even better than the boots Dylan had imagined because he could see the length of leg encased in sheer black tights.

Fortunately, Jane was leaning into the vehicle to fold down seats and didn't see the appreciative scan Dylan gave her body so he was surprised to see a vaguely embarrassed expression on her face when she emerged.

'My Beemer's in the garage,' she muttered. 'Good guess.'

He shrugged. 'Not that hard. Not after you handed me a gold credit card and told me to go crazy in the baby shop this morning.'

'Did you get everything you think you might need?'

'I reckon. The big stuff, anyway. Cot and stroller and front pack and blankets. And look— this was a free gift.' Dylan carefully fished a small item from his pocket.

'What is it?'

'A headband.' Dylan let the soft loop of cotton

knit unfold to hang in a circle from his finger. 'A Christmas headband.'

Jane gave the white band with its embroidered holly leaves and red berries a dismissive glance. 'It's only November.'

It wouldn't have made any difference if it was the last week of December, would it? Christmas festivities and frivolities clearly had no place in Dr Walters's life. They were probably deemed a nuisance that created clutter and interfered with smooth routines.

'No harm in being prepared,' he said mildly. 'And it looked very bonny when she tried it on. The girls in the shop said it was the cutest thing they'd ever seen. They were very helpful girls.'

Jane raised an eyebrow. 'I'm sure.'

Dylan ignored the innuendo. 'I'm assuming this place we're going to has shops that will have baby food?'

She nodded. 'Akaroa's a top tourist destination. Along with all the gourmet restaurants and boutique shopping, you'll find a supermarket and pharmacy. There are doctors and even a small hospital if it's needed.'

'Great. Maybe I can get a job.'

She looked alarmed now. 'I didn't think you were intending to stay that long. And, anyway, who would look after Sophie?'

At least she had used the baby's name for once. One step forward, two back?

'I'll bring the gear out. I got the delivery chaps to leave it all downstairs in the foyer. Some old lady gave me a very disapproving look, I have to say.'

'That must have been Mrs Connell. From downstairs. Do you need some help?'

'Yes. Here, you take Sophie.'

'But I—'

Dylan didn't allow time for an excuse to be expressed. He pressed the well-wrapped baby bundle against Jane's chest and she was forced to put her arms around it, her eyes widening enough to make her look shocked at his assertiveness.

He was slightly shocked himself. Not by his insistence on her holding the baby but by the way his body was reacting to that inadvertent brush of his hands against Jane's breasts. Dammit! He knew that tingle.

Moving quickly, Dylan embarked on the task

of loading his purchases into the back of the vehicle. He wasn't here to get attracted to Sophie's genetic mother. No way! Not only was she completely not his type of woman, he was on a mission that was quite complicated enough already.

Sophie had started crying by the time Dylan was slotting the three-wheeled stroller on top of the boxes that contained the kit-set cot. She was howling as he put in a cane bassinette stuffed with baby linen and blankets. With the last load of a plastic bath, changing mat and supply of baby wipes, it was clear that Jane was nearly as upset as the baby. It was time to rescue her.

'She hates me,' Jane said flatly as Dylan took the bundle. She pointed the remote at the vehicle and locked the doors. 'I need to get changed.'

She walked off into the apartment building without a backward glance.

Dylan looked down at the tiny red face. 'You're not helping,' he said sadly. 'Give her a chance, eh? It's what she's giving *us*.'

She was. She had agreed that her penthouse apartment was totally unsuitable for an infant.

She had offered what seemed like an ideal alternative. A fully furnished holiday house in a small town beside a beach. A private place where they would have the opportunity to talk. He could stay there as long as he liked. As long as it took to sort out the best thing to do. Perfect. Or so it had seemed until he'd thought about it some more. This small settlement was certainly far enough away for Jane not to be distracted by domestic or professional concerns but maybe it was a bit *too* far away. Maybe he and Sophie were being neatly shunted aside.

Out of sight and out of mind?

He needed to work on that. Jane was going to stay in Akaroa with them for tonight, at least. Dylan hoped inspiration might strike by then.

It would need to!

Tucked into her car seat and sound asleep, Sophie could have been on another planet as far as Jane seemed concerned on their drive to her country residence a short time later. She seemed more interested in giving Dylan a history lesson.

'We're heading southeast,' she informed him as they left the city behind. 'This is Bank's peninsula, which was actually sold to a captain of a French whaling ship back in the 1830s or so. If the French had got their act together a bit more quickly, New Zealand could have been theirs instead of under British sovereignty.'

'Is that so?' While it was interesting, Dylan wanted a rather more personal conversation. 'What's your connection?'

'My grandmother was a descendent of one of the early settlers. The street her cottage is on is actually named after her family. Number three, Rue Brabant.'

'Rue? As in French for street?'

'Akaroa is New Zealand's only French settlement. It's got a very distinctive feel to it and they hang on to the heritage from the first settlers.'

'And you inherited the cottage from your grandmother?'

'No. It went to her daughter. My mother.'

This was alarming. Was Jane taking him and Sophie to stay with her mother? An older and potentially more fierce version of Jane?

She flicked him a glance. 'Don't worry. Mum's

not there. She only ever went to the cottage for the odd weekend and she died quite a few years ago now. Not long after she retired.'

'Oh, I'm sorry. And your father?'

'Also dead.'

'But…' Dylan frowned. 'Can I ask a personal question?'

'You can ask. I don't guarantee I'll answer it.'

'How old are you, Jane?'

'Thirty-five. Why?'

'Your parents must have died very young.'

'Not tragically. Dad was in his early sixties. Mum got to seventy.'

'But…' Dylan was confused now. 'You're only thirty-five and it's been how long since your mum died?'

'I was what you might call a change-of-life baby,' Jane said reluctantly. 'Mum was forty-three when I came along.'

'Oh.' Dylan tucked the information away because it seemed important. After a glance over his shoulder to check that Sophie was happy and a look out the windows to admire the flat farmland around them, he decided it was worth trying for some more information. Knowledge was power, after all.

'My mum died of pneumonia,' he offered. 'She'd always had lung problems. What happened to your folks?'

'Dad killed himself by working too hard. Kind of ironic, because he was a cardiologist and he had a massive MI.'

'And your mother?'

'She was a neurologist. She retired at sixty-seven and I think she died of boredom. Her work had been her life and she never found anything interesting enough to replace the passion.'

'So you're an orphan,' Dylan said sympathetically. 'Just like wee Sophie.'

Oops. There was no mistaking the way Jane's fingers tightened on the steering-wheel. Or the way her mouth compressed itself into a thin line that let him know he had said the wrong thing.

Dylan tried to make amends. 'Your parents sound like impressive people.'

That was better. Jane nodded approvingly as they passed a sign naming a small settlement as Cooptown and she slowed the car.

'They were,' she said proudly. 'They were both devoted to their work and highly respected.'

'You were an only child?'

'Yes.'

'A surprise?' The query was cautious but Jane didn't seem offended.

'That's what change-of-life babies usually are, aren't they? My parents were delighted once they got used to the idea, of course.'

'But they had their important careers well established. I don't suppose they found too much time for family stuff.'

'My parents were wonderful people,' Jane said stiffly. 'They loved me and I loved them. Yes, they both had busy careers but they did their best for me.'

But it hadn't been enough, had it? However determined Jane was to put a brave face on it, he could hear the wistful tone of a lonely young girl somewhere beneath those words. His next question was gentle.

'You had a nanny?'

'Yes. She was a lovely woman.'

'And you went to boarding schools?'

'Very good schools. I was happy.'

Now she sounded defensive. Dylan simply made a sound that indicated he'd heard what she'd said and then he fell silent as they began driving uphill. The silence ticked on and then Jane sighed.

'All right. What's the point you're trying to make?'

She knew. But maybe it was time to get it out into the open. 'I suspect your experience has made you believe that having a professional career and being a good mother are not compatible.'

Jane snorted. 'Thanks, Sigmund. I could have worked that one out for myself, you know.'

'It doesn't *have* to be like that.' Was Jane being so defensive because she felt in conflict? Did a part of her like the idea of being a mother? Even if it was a tiny part, it was worth encouraging.

'With the kind of career I have, it does.' Jane was negotiating tight bends, easing the heavy vehicle up the steep, narrow road with impressive ease. 'You can't be there to cheer on a race at a school sports day if you're rostered on in an operating theatre. Or clap at prizegiving if you happen to be delivering a keynote speech at a conference in Milan. Or watch the candles being blown out on a birthday cake if you're on call and your pager goes off. Or…'

Jane took a deep breath as she negotiated the next bend. Then she shook her head. 'So many things. Not important on their own but they add up. It isn't a good mix for anyone involved. I know. End of story.'

A sad story. Dylan could hear the pain of a lonely child. Hungry for her parents' attention. Had that been why she had followed them into the same profession? Seeking approval and common ground?

Was the sense of deprivation deep enough for her to not wish it on someone else?

Like her own child?

It was Dylan's turn to sigh. He hadn't expected a barrier this solid. Maybe he'd done the wrong thing coming here at all, but he couldn't have known. He still couldn't know what was really going on in Jane's head—or, more important—her heart. She was having to face things she had probably considered long buried. A non-issue.

She had to be feeling at least some level of confusion.

On top of that, she had to be hurting for the loss of a close friend. She'd been crying before he'd turned up at her apartment last night. She might not want to share her feelings but that didn't mean they weren't overwhelming. So much so that it might be impossible for her to be thinking rationally about the future.

About Sophie.

She needed time and that was fine. Sophie's future hung in the balance here and he needed time as well. He needed to get to know this woman a little better. He wasn't about to try and persuade Jane to have a huge influence in the life of his niece if it wasn't going to be the very best option available.

Dylan had stopped talking, both to gather his own thoughts and in the hope that the tense atmosphere in the car would diffuse, but as they reached the top of the huge hill they'd been climbing, he couldn't stay silent any longer.

'Holy heck!' he exclaimed. 'Would you look at that?'

Jane was smiling as she pulled off the road into the car park of a building labelled the Hilltop Tavern. She parked facing the view that had just taken Dylan's breath away.

Far ahead, past the spectacular rolling green of hills and valleys, was the brilliant blue of a harbour, with more hills seeming to roll into it, leaving an irregular coastline and projections that whispered of hidden bays and private beaches.

Dylan had to get out of the car. To shield his eyes and simply stare for several long minutes. It was easy to ignore the sparse evidence of human habitation. This land looked, for the most part, untouched. Perfect.

'It's gorgeous, isn't it?' Jane spoke quietly from just behind his right shoulder. 'I never get tired of this view. It's worth driving up that horrible road.'

'It's the most beautiful place I've ever seen,' Dylan decreed. He turned so that he could look directly at Jane. 'Thank you for bringing me here.'

She loved this place. He could see that she was

really pleased by his response to seeing it and, for the first time, Dylan felt the tiniest connection with this woman. Something they could agree on and share.

What a shame it had nothing to do with the baby still happily asleep in the back seat of the car behind them.

Still, Dylan felt happier as he climbed back into the vehicle. How could he not, as the drive into that magical landscape continued? Past remote houses and challenging-looking farmland. Past a cheese factory and along a delightful stretch of coastline with boat sheds and ramps and children playing. Into Akaroa village, which was picturesque enough not to be a disappointment after that fabulous view from the hilltop.

'I love it,' Dylan said, as they drove to the other side of the village. 'The street signs, the lighthouse, that cute jetty house with its turret roof. The French flags. Everything!'

'It's different, isn't it? A lot of artists and alternative lifestylers are drawn to live here.' Jane turned up a tiny, steep street and drove very slowly. 'You should feel right at home.'

'Sorry? I'm a nurse, not an artist.'

'I just meant…' Jane was blushing again as she parked the car. Had he really thought this woman had icy self-control? 'Well, you're… different.'

'Am I?' Dylan wasn't sure he liked that. Or was it a good thing? He wanted it to be a good thing. He needed it to be, for Sophie's sake. 'How?'

Jane bit her lip. 'Honestly?'

'Aye.' If they couldn't be honest with each other, they weren't going to get anywhere.

'When I first saw you—in ED yesterday—I thought you looked like…um…a gypsy. And that you might be happier holding a guitar instead of a baby.'

She looked up and Dylan was astonished to see shyness in her expression. It was unexpected. And appealing. And her eyes *were* an extraordinary colour. Not quite green but not quite hazel. Unique.

Intriguing.

He let the silence hang for just another second. Long enough to enjoy that expression and those eyes and to anticipate a new connection that might build on what they had already achieved so far today.

He smiled.

'I love my guitar,' he confessed. 'Good guess.'

CHAPTER FIVE

HE WAS doing it again.

Smiling at her.

Jane had never seen a smile quite like Dylan's. It made her feel as if she had somehow made him very happy and, curiously, it seemed to make *her* feel just as good.

Very, very good. Right down to her bones.

Weird, considering that his reference back to her 'good guess' confirmed they were complete opposites. She had a BMW convertible in her garage for when she had the rare moment free to enjoy it. He loved his guitar and probably sat for hours making music.

The old adage that opposites attracted filtered into Jane's brain.

No! That was absurd.

He just had a lovely smile, that was all. One that had the ability to draw you into a moment of time that had nothing to do with anything else that might be happening in your life.

Like a stressful job and the grief of losing your best friend and the shock of being presented with a live baby and…

And she had to remember all these things and not get lost in a smile to the point of imagining herself to be attracted to this man. It was much easier once she dragged her gaze away from his face and moved so it couldn't find its way back. She got out of the car and waited by the wooden gate in the hedge while Dylan unhooked the car seat containing Sophie and picked up her bag of supplies.

'I must apologise for the mess here,' she said briskly. 'I had a gardener who used to look after the place but he had a mild stroke about three months ago and can't work any longer. I haven't found the time to do anything about employing anyone else.'

Dylan put out a hand to shield Sophie from the drooping fronds of the hawthorn hedge. Big hands, Jane noticed. With long fingers that she could easily imagine plucking the strings of a guitar. The protection of the infant he carried was clearly automatic with no thought being given to the scratches he might receive himself from the sharp thorns. It was nice to know he was good at looking after something helpless. A perfect guardian.

Aware that Dylan was watching her, Jane hastily averted her gaze again and put her shoulder against the gate. The hinges were rusty and the hedge was doing its best to swallow the opening.

'Dinna fesh yourself,' Dylan was saying as he followed her up the narrow cobbled path where rose branches reached out to try and attack their legs. 'It's…'

Jane turned to see that he'd stopped and was staring at the house. Sophie was whimpering but the sound didn't seem to have penetrated Dylan's consciousness yet. She turned back, trying to see past the necessary tasks she had been mentally cataloguing, like pruning the roses and mowing the lawns and clearing out the guttering. Trying to see what Dylan was seeing that could make his expression an echo of what it had been on the hilltop when he'd caught sight of the landscape.

The cottage was well over a hundred years old. The dark grey corrugated-iron roof was steeply pitched, edged with ornately carved barge-boards. There were tall brick chimneys with fancy clay pots on the top and dormer windows, divided into small squares, in each of the three gables. A long, bull-nosed veranda roof ran the whole width of the lower storey and, currently, the wisteria vine that hung from its iron lace was profusely in bloom.

Long delicate blue flowers hung to almost touch the flowers of the lavender hedge running wild below. You could only catch a glimpse of the wicker furniture on the veranda and the French doors and windows of the house beyond.

It certainly looked invitingly shady, given the brilliance and surprising heat of the sunshine they were standing in. It *was* pretty, Jane conceded. Even in this disreputable state. She had been coming to this house for as long as she could remember and she had always loved it.

'It's gorgeous.' Dylan bestowed another smile

on her as he finally finished his sentence. 'It's the bonniest wee house I've ever seen.'

'Come on in.' Jane concentrated on locating the correct key on the ring. She didn't want to try and analyse why Dylan's response to this property made her feel like the connection she'd felt when he smiled at her had just increased tenfold.

He loved the house, that was all. Lots of people adored old houses and a man like Dylan was bound to be drawn to a dwelling that looked so free from the constraints of tidiness. It wasn't that he understood why this patch of land and its buildings had been so special in Jane's life. The place of time out in school holidays. Of home baking and cuddles and someone to whom she was more important than anything else.

'It might be a bit musty inside,' she warned as she unlocked the door. 'I'll turn the power and water on. We can get the coal range going later but I'll go down to the bakery first. It's way past time for some lunch. You must be starving.'

'Pretty hungry,' Dylan admitted. 'I'll feed wee Sophie first, though.'

Yes. He was a good guardian. Jane didn't need to feel guilty at the prospect of allowing her offspring to be raised by a more distant genetic relative.

Still, she hesitated, having shown Dylan into the farm-style kitchen that took up nearly half the ground floor of the house and turned on the main switch so that the microwave and other appliances would be functional.

'Do you need any help?'

Dylan seemed to consider the offer carefully. 'I can manage for now,' he decided. 'Your plan for some lunch sounded good.'

'There's instant coffee and tea in those canisters but I'll have to pick up some milk.'

A tin of formula had appeared on the wooden bench top that surrounded an ancient ceramic sink. Then Dylan put a bottle beside it.

'There's a rocking chair out on the veranda.' Jane still felt the urge to assist in some way. 'It might be a nice place to feed her while it's sunny.'

Dylan smiled and Jane was aware of a sudden need to escape. 'I won't be long,' she promised.

She wasn't. When she returned less than thirty minutes later with bags full of supplies, she found Dylan in the spot she had recommended. She saw him before he spotted her coming up the path and Jane's step slowed unconsciously. Part of her wanted to stop and freeze-frame this moment in time but she knew it was an image she would never forget, however short it was in reality.

Dylan sat in the rocking chair with Sophie in the crook of one arm. He held her bottle in his other hand but the baby looked as if she was trying to help, with a tiny hand on top of one of Dylan's fingers. She was staring up at the man who held her while she sucked on the bottle, and Dylan was looking down. The sense of communion between the two of them was so powerful that Jane felt totally excluded.

She didn't want to be included in Sophie's life to the extent of having that kind of a bond so why did she feel as though she was missing something? Something…huge.

Maybe it was because they were *here* and so many of the good things in her childhood were associated with this house. That veranda. That rocking chair, even. The distant and long-forgotten memory of sitting on her grandmother's knee and being rocked to a state of blissful fantasy as she listened to a story being read was poignant enough to bring tears to Jane's eyes.

Good grief! She was turning into an emotional train wreck! Demonstrating the kind of feminine weakness that had never been allowed in her life. Weeping uncontrollably at frequent intervals was as unthinkable as…as being a mother!

Dylan had seen her now. Hopefully he hadn't seen the way she was blinking so hard but, in any case, it was Sophie he spoke to.

'She's back,' he said softly, making it sound as if Jane's arrival was the exciting occurrence they'd both been anticipating. 'And I think there might be some food for me in those bags.'

'There is.' Jane could do something helpful now. Something pleasingly nurturing, even. 'I've got fresh bread and milk. Ham and cheese and biscuits and fruit.'

Dylan put the bottle down and shifted the baby so that she was over his shoulder. He began to rub her back and even though she managed to start climbing the steps to the veranda, Jane couldn't look away from that big hand moving so gently on the tiny body.

Then Sophie gave a very unladylike belch and Dylan glanced up to catch Jane's gaze. They both grinned.

And Jane had the strangest sensation of falling. She actually put a hand out to touch a veranda post to make sure she didn't end up flat on her face.

'I'll…um…get some coffee brewing, shall I?'

'Please.' Dylan was holding her gaze. 'With fresh coffee and a ham sarnie, I'll be yours to command, Dr Walters.'

There was no reason to blush. Or avert her gaze hastily as if she was being coy. What on earth was happening to her?

Jane escaped into the house. She set food out on the antique kauri table, collecting plates and cutlery from the matching hutch dresser with such determined efficiency she almost dropped one of her gran's lovely old blue and white china cups. While the coffee was percolating, she rushed through the lower level of the house, throwing windows open to let in the sunshine and fresh air.

And, hopefully, a bit of common sense.

He stayed right where he was. Holding a baby heavy with contentment, in the dappled shade of the veranda. Dylan was aware of the creak of the rocking chair on old wooden boards, the call of birds in the trees and the snuffling sounds of the small creature in his arms. He could smell the subtle fragrance of the glorious blue flowers that wept from the vine above his head and the uniquely baby smell of Sophie.

He needed a moment here.

Time to let his mind flick back a minute or two. To when he'd seen Jane coming down the narrow brick path with a bag in her arms that had a long stick of crusty, French bread poking from the top.

The sleeves of her soft white shirt had been rolled up and it was tucked into jeans that were probably some designer brand judging by the way they fitted like a second skin. The legs of the jeans had been rolled up too and the sandals and bare toes had made it look as though Jane was heading for a beach.

It wasn't just the clothing that had made her seem so different, however. Or the way the wind had teased wispy curls from the fancy braid on the back of her head. The feeling of a shift in perspective had gone way deeper than that.

For just a heartbeat, it had felt like Jane was no longer a stranger. As though he had always known her. That this wasn't the first time he'd been here, sitting like this and watching for her return. That it wouldn't be the last time, either, because this was where he was meant to be.

This was *home*.

The odd sensation had only lasted a moment but it was disturbingly easy to recall.

Fortunately, it was just as easy to dismiss.

It was…ludicrous.

How could this feel like home when it was completely unlike anything he'd ever associated with home? Not that he remembered much of his own mother because he'd been too young when she had been torn from his life, but what he did remember was engraved on his heart.

Instinctively, Dylan changed his grip on Sophie as he remembered the soft voice and the cuddles. The smell of home baking. The safety of knowing she would always be there. When he woke up in the night or came home from school. When he was feeling sick or had grazed his knees falling from his bike. Her praise had been a coveted prize and her touch had had the power to heal. Her songs and laughter had been music he could still catch occasionally, like a fairy whisper.

Dylan pressed a soft, lingering kiss to the downy fluff on Sophie's head.

That was the kind of mother he would wish for this precious child.

Jane's touch could heal, he reminded himself. And he could be confident that she cared about her young patients. Enough to dedicate her life to their well-being, in fact, but it wasn't the same. It wasn't enough because… Why? Because it felt empty?

Distant?

Yes. That was the key. Real emotional connection was missing. The kind of love that was selfless and so pure that it became more important than life itself. A mother's love.

Power-dressing Dr Walters, the ultimate professional with an apartment sterile enough to rival an operating theatre and a prestigious sports car in her garage couldn't be further from the ideal.

Couldn't be more wrong. Was he dreaming to think that, given time, Jane might find a real connection with her biological child? Was he expecting magic?

With a sigh, Dylan eased himself from the rocking chair and went inside.

He made a nest for Sophie on an old rolled-arm couch in a living area that was separated from the kitchen by an open archway. He could see Jane in there, busy at the kitchen bench, as he crouched to make sure Sophie would be safe within her wall of cushions. The baby lay on her side, wrapped snugly in her fuzzy blanket, one tiny fist pressed against her nose. Gently, Dylan moved the hand.

'Don't want you scratching your beautiful wee nose, hinny,' he murmured. His fingertip brushed the deep dimple on the top of the little button nose. Dark eyelashes fluttered and the corner of Sophie's mouth lifted in what looked like a smile.

Dylan was certainly smiling as he straightened. He found himself looking at a crowded bookshelf and the smile faded. He felt his heart miss a beat as he experienced another flash of that curious feeling of having been here before.

It was just the books, he told himself. The same books his mother had treasured. *Anne of Green Gables* and *Little Women* and *Heidi*. Classics anyone might have. Even old, well-loved copies like these that had plain, rubbed covers in muted shades of moss green and dusty pink.

Maybe it had something to do with the clutter of photographs as well. On top of the bookshelf and the mantelpiece of the open fireplace and the upright piano in the corner. Photographs of people. Of family.

Many wore graduation gowns. Formal portraits to celebrate academic achievement, but some were less formal. Like that one of a woman holding an infant. Dylan stepped close to the piano and picked up the photograph in its silver frame.

The baby was older than Sophie. Maybe nine or ten months. She had big, round eyes and a gorgeous smile, but what caught Dylan's attention enough to make him catch his breath was the baby's nose. A little button of a nose with an obvious dimple on the top.

His stride was almost urgent as he entered the kitchen.

'Is this you?' he demanded.

Jane's eyes widened. She stared at Dylan for a long moment before dropping her gaze to the photograph clutched in his hand.

'Yes.' She looked up again. Wary.

'Your nose!' Dylan couldn't help the stupid grin that tugged at his lips.

'What's wrong with it?' Jane was frowning now.

'Nothing. It's a very bonny nose.'

Jane took a step back. She gave her head a tiny disbelieving shake and then pulled a serrated bread knife from the wooden block beside the cooker.

'It's the dimple,' Dylan explained patiently. 'It's identical to Sophie's. She's got *your* nose, Jane.'

She took another glance. 'It's a baby nose,' she said dismissively. 'They all have dimples.'

Dylan's grin died and his hand lowered as he

watched Jane deftly slicing the loaf of bread. He knew she was wrong but refuting that confident tone could only lead to strife. Judging by the way she was attacking the bread, she was not someone who liked to come off second best from any confrontation. And maybe she wasn't wrong. She did have more experience with babies than he did.

It seemed politic to change the subject.

'Lunch looks good.' Even if it didn't show any evidence of home baking.

'The food here is wonderful.' Jane nodded, piling the bread slices into a basket lined with a blue and white gingham cloth. 'And some of the restaurants will do their meals as take-outs. We could do that for dinner.'

No home cooking on offer, either. Dylan put the photograph face down on the hutch dresser that had a collection of fine old blue and white china.

'Take a seat,' Jane directed. 'Lunch is ready if you are.'

You couldn't describe her voice as soft, Dylan noted as he sat down at the table. It had a clarity and energy about it that made you think of authority figures. A headmistress perhaps. Or a

CEO. Nothing like his image of a mother's voice. And as for cuddles…

He couldn't help raking a glance over Jane as she turned to join him at the table. That open-necked white shirt was unbuttoned far enough to reveal a hint of cleavage. In the moment before she'd turned, he'd already registered the way her jeans covered a neat backside. Apple cheeks he could probably cover completely with his hands. She'd given up on that plait in her hair now, too. It hung in loose waves to her shoulders.

Dylan pulled in a breath.

No. Jane could not be deemed cuddly. She was…hot, dammit!

He pulled in another breath.

Jane stared at him. 'Are you all right?'

'I'm fine.'

'You're not asthmatic or something?'

'No. Why?'

'You seem short of breath.'

'Healthy as a horse,' Dylan muttered. 'And hungry enough to eat one.'

* * *

Jane watched him eat. Piling ham and cheese and tomatoes onto lengths of the split loaf of bread. Clearly enjoying the food she had prepared.

It felt good.

Disturbingly good, because it should feel like an intrusion, having a stranger here. Sitting at this table. This was her retreat. A place like none other in her world. A private place where she could unfailingly—if only intermittently—find real contentment. And she hadn't exactly chosen to invite these guests. It felt like it had been entirely Dylan's idea.

Maybe it didn't feel like an invasion because of the way Dylan was reacting to everything. She had seen him begin to fall under the spell of this tiny patch of the globe from the instant he'd first seen it. He was falling in love with it. A stranger who had no previous association with her life. He had no reason to think it odd that she had such a bond with an old, cluttered cottage miles from anywhere, so maybe that was why he seemed to…understand.

When they had finished their lunch and Jane

was tidying the kitchen, he picked up a tea towel and dried dishes, and he handled Gran's china with the kind of respect it deserved. He wiped down the table as Jane was putting leftover food away in the refrigerator and, out of the corner of her eye, she saw the way he ran his fingers over the pitted surface and moulded edge. As though he could sense its history. The times when food had been served with love and shared with laughter.

He looked far too big when he followed Jane up the narrow staircase to see the two bedrooms upstairs.

'That's my room,' Jane said. 'You and Sophie will have to share this one.'

It was only a step across the tiny hallway from her own. Close enough for the thought of sleeping in such proximity to bring warmth to Jane's cheeks.

'If that's OK,' she added hurriedly.

'OK?' Dylan had to duck his head a little to go through the doorway. He looked at the ancient double brass bed covered with one of Gran's patchwork quilts. His gaze moved to the Scotch chest with the old enamel basin and pitcher and then he moved closer to Jane, who was standing by the window with its tiny built-in seat and a view that overlooked the rambling garden. When he lifted his gaze, Jane knew he would be looking at the sea and the jetty with its quaint little structure on the end and the lighthouse she loved further round the bay.

He turned his head to Jane then and she watched the smile grow on his face. She could feel it as well as see it. It stretched inside her chest, reaching out to touch her heart.

'It's not OK,' he said. 'It's perfect, hinny. This place is like something out of a fairy-tale.'

Hinny. The odd endearment she had heard him use for Sophie. He shouldn't be using it on her. And it certainly shouldn't be making her feel so delighted. And it wasn't. She was just pleased that he appreciated the view.

Her nod of acknowledgement was curt. She shouldn't be feeling this pleased. It would be dangerous to start enjoying the company of this man. Maybe it had been a mistake to bring him here. She had seen it as a way out of an impossible situation. A reprieve. And, yes, it had occurred to her that this place might suit the gypsy man.

She just hadn't realised how well it would suit him. For a crazy moment it felt like this was *his* home.

That he belonged here.

But he didn't. And neither did his baby.

'Might be a tight squeeze,' she pointed out briskly. 'For the cot and everything.'

'It's perfect,' Dylan repeated, his accent curling around the word, making it sound as though this was all anyone could wish for. 'Thank you for bringing us here, Jane.'

He smiled at her.

It took a conscious effort to pull in a breath.

'It's a bit stuffy in here, isn't it?' Jane tugged on the brass fitting on the bottom of the sash window but it refused to budge. She tugged harder. Then she transferred her grip to the underside of the wooden frame but the window resisted her effort to open it.

'Let me.' Dylan's hands brushed hers as he reached for the sash. The window creaked in protest but rose a few inches.

'It hasn't been opened for a while.' Jane's hands were beside her now. Clenched into fists. It had been a shock, that sharp tingle of Dylan's touch. Had it worn off? Experimentally, she opened them and flexed her fingers.

'Easily fixed.' Dylan's gaze flicked down. 'You didn't hurt yourself, did you?'

'No.'

But it was too late. Dylan had picked up her hand to examine it. Her fingers lay on top of his and his thumb was brushing over them, checking for sign of injury.

Pull it away, Jane told herself. Move. This is…not good.

Like an echo of her own unease, a faint wail filtered up the stairs. Sophie was awake.

Jane snatched her hand back. 'I'm fine,' she assured Dylan. 'And I think you're being summoned.'

Keeping busy was the answer, Jane remembered. It had worked before, when she'd been getting lunch ready, and it could work again. She aired the beds and tidied and dusted, keeping a good distance from Dylan as he attended to changing and feeding the baby, putting the cot together and unpacking and sorting all the gear he had purchased that morning.

She was dusting the photographs on the piano when he laid out a colourful quilted mat on the living-room floor. It had padded arches over the top with bright, soft toy animals that dangled with pompom feet on string legs. He laid Sophie on the mat to look up at the animals and Jane had to smile as she heard the gurgle of delight and saw the way those tiny hands moved.

It was disconcerting, however, to see Dylan sprawl on the floor beside the baby and roll onto his back with his head right beside the mat, so that he could see what she was seeing.

'There's a lion,' she heard him whisper. 'Can you see, hinny? And a wee monkey. And a heffalump.'

A heffalump? Good grief! Jane hadn't heard an elephant called that since...since the murmured stories she had listened to on her gran's lap.

Sudden tears came from nowhere again and stung the backs of her eyes. She struggled to contain them, ignoring the photograph she had knocked over with the duster.

'I'm going outside,' she announced. 'There's just a bit of daylight left and I should see what needs doing in the garden.'

Dylan propped himself up on one elbow. 'I could do that,' he offered.

'You're busy.'

'I didn't mean right now. I meant…while I'm here. I'll have plenty of time.'

How long was 'plenty'? Jane wondered. How long was he planning to be here? Long enough for her to get used to having him around? To *want* him to stay around?

She shook her head. 'It's a huge job. It's so overgrown out there, I can't even see the gazebo that's down past the fruit trees. I need to get someone in to deal with the heavy stuff.'

'You don't have the tools? Clippers and a spade and suchlike?'

'I have tools. There's a shed. But—'

'But nothing.' Dylan sat up and then rose with a remarkably fluid motion for such a large man. He stepped towards Jane and he was frowning.

'I came here to let you meet your daughter,' he said without preamble. 'I'm not about to introduce you and then whisk her away. We all need time and you've given us a perfect place for that. I don't suppose you were planning to ask me for rent for this accommodation?'

'Of course not!' The idea was somehow insulting.

'There you go, then. I don't take handouts.' His pride was obvious in the way he held his head and the challenging look she was being given. 'I'll pay my way,' he continued. 'I can fix things like that window upstairs. And the gate. And I can tidy the garden. It would be my pleasure,' he added, his tone softening. 'A privilege, even.'

His eyes were so dark it should have been hard to read his expression but Jane could see sincerity there. And…a plea? Was he asking to be useful? More a part of her life? To feel like he belonged?

Dangerous.

But…practical, for heaven's sake. She was reading too much into this. Reacting oddly. He needed a place to stay. She needed the garden tidied. It was an arrangement that would obviously suit them both. Especially her.

Having Dylan and Sophie here put them completely outside the sphere of Jane's everyday life. A life she fully intended to return to tomorrow. It would give her all the time she needed to get her head around the situation and find a solution.

'Sounds fair,' she finally said slowly. 'If you're sure you want to.'

'I want to.'

'If you change your mind, it won't matter. I can always get someone in to finish the job.'

She couldn't look away from him. She needed to get outside and find some new air.

'I never leave a job half-done,' Dylan said quietly. 'I'll be here for as long as it takes, Jane.'

There was nothing more to be said. All Jane could do was nod and turn back to her task. She picked up the photograph that had been knocked over. Was it coincidence that it was the one Dylan had taken into the kitchen earlier? Jane stared at the baby in the picture. At her nose.

Her hand seemed to move of its own accord. Reaching up so that she could touch her own grown-up nose. To feel the dimple she'd always disliked.

She wasn't about to stare at the real baby in the room and make comparisons to the photograph, however. Jane's step did not falter as she headed back to the kitchen to make a shopping list of what they'd need for dinner.

She didn't want to find a similarity. A connection.

She simply couldn't afford to.

CHAPTER SIX

DARKNESS closed around the little cottage, cutting off the rest of the world and making the atmosphere inside a lot more...intimate.

Jane cleared away after their dinner while Dylan found everything he needed for Sophie's bath. The meal they had just shared had impressed them both. A local French restaurant had provided a superb beef bourguignon and scalloped potatoes. Jane had made a fresh garden salad and added newly baked ciabatta bread from the Italian bakery. The prize-winning Merlot she had chosen to accompany the meal had been the perfect finishing touch.

Or had that been the candles she had impulsively placed on the table?

Whatever. The rich food and wine and the

candlelight making Gran's precious old silver and crystal sparkle, along with the warmth from the fire now glowing in the living room's open fireplace and some of her favourite music playing softly in the background had made it the most enjoyable meal Jane could remember having in ages.

Ever, even.

Dylan had been amazed by the music.

'Vinyl!' he had exclaimed. 'Nobody still has a record player. This place really is magic. I'm in a time warp!'

'Gran loved music,' Jane had said defensively. 'She bought the best stereo she could find at the time and it still works perfectly well. I've never felt the need to update the technology here.'

Dylan had sifted through the pile. 'Treasure.' He'd grinned. 'I've found Simon and Garfunkel. Cat Stevens. Good Lord—The Seekers?'

'Hey! There's nothing wrong with The Seekers. It's great music.'

Dylan had been smiling as he'd placed the vinyl disc on the turntable and lowered the needle mechanism. Then he'd looked up and something in that smile had made Jane's throat feel curiously tight.

He knew every one of those songs, she discovered as Sophie slept in her cane bassinette beside the table and they discussed music as they ate. He had learned to play his guitar with those songs and they were part of his soul. Pure joy.

When talk turned to books, they had read and loved the same authors and when the conversation included movies, it was obvious how similar all their tastes were. Jane began to feel spooked.

She was trying to analyse her reaction as she washed and dried the dishes. How could someone like Dylan seem so compatible when he was so unlike any man she had ever been interested in?

Never mind that relationships in the past had always ended on a faintly sour note. Jane was still very clear about her tick list. He had to be a professional man. At least her equal in the medical hierarchy. Dylan wasn't even on the bottom rung of the same ladder.

It had to be someone who could understand and share her passion for her career. Dylan was a free spirit. He could pick up his job wherever he happened to be and then move on to new ground. You couldn't progress in your career that way.

Her ideal man also had a sharp wit and the intelligence to provide stimulating conversation about things that mattered. She and Dylan hadn't discussed anything that could be considered important during their meal. Not a word about medicine or politics or even current affairs. They had talked about entertainment, for heaven's sake. Personal preferences in the frivolous world of fiction and music.

So why on earth had she enjoyed it so much? Why was she left with this echo of animated conversation and laughter that was so pleasant it made her yearn for more of the same?

Weird.

Jane slotted the last plate onto the rack on the hutch dresser and turned to snuff out the candles. She took the last of her glass of wine with her when she went to put another log on the fire and change the record. Because it was a Saturday night and she didn't have to work tomorrow or even drive until later in the day, Jane decided to refill her glass when it was empty. When she returned to the kitchen to find the bottle, she saw that Dylan had placed the plastic baby bath on a towel on the old table and was filling it with jugs of warm water from the tap over the sink.

Somehow, she ended up staying in there. Leaning against the bench, sipping her wine and watching him bath Sophie.

His feet were bare beneath the jeans he was wearing and his T-shirt left his arms bare. Well-muscled arms with a covering of fine dark hair and those large hands with long fingers seemed absolutely enormous with a tiny naked baby beneath them.

The strength in those muscles was obvious. Jane could so easily imagine them outside, in her overgrown garden, bulging and twisting as Dylan broke through heavy earth by swinging a pickaxe or pulled up an unwanted shrub or self-sown tree by its roots. Yet here they were, holding that small, fragile body afloat in deep, warm water. Smoothing shampoo onto the fuzzy scalp and then rinsing it clean by scooping palms full of water to cup the baby's head.

It was mesmerising to watch the movements. His touch. Sophie seemed to find it equally enthralling. She lay quite still in the water, with just the occasional kick of her legs or wave of her arms. Was she watching the way his hair curled around his face as he bent over her? The movement of his lips as he talked reassuring nonsense? Maybe Dylan's smile had the same effect on Sophie as it seemed to have on her. Making her feel special.

Loved.

Jane swallowed. Hard. She picked up her wine and went back to the living room to curl up on one end of the battered leather couch in front of the fire. To listen to the music instead of the soft rumble of Dylan's voice. To get away from whatever it was that was pulling her somewhere she really didn't want to go.

'Time for bed, lassie.'

Dylan rose from the kitchen chair where he had given Sophie her last bottle of formula for the day. She had obligingly expelled any air in her tummy and she would, hopefully, settle soon in the bassinette he had put upstairs in his bedroom. Maybe tonight she would even sleep through until dawn.

He adjusted the sweet-smelling bundle so that the baby's head nestled against his chest just below his collarbone, and he began to walk, humming along with the folk music playing softly from that astonishing old record player.

The kitchen was quite small and Dylan's monotonous circuit drew him a little further into the living area each time he passed the archway. Jane was sitting in there, on the couch by the fire, with her legs tucked up. She held her glass of wine and seemed to be staring dreamily at the flames licking a fresh log of wood.

His humming took on a satisfied note. He'd made the right choice, he applauded himself, in not pushing Jane to get involved with the care of wee Sophie today. For now, it was enough that they were all together. That Jane seemed to be accepting the presence of the new arrival in her life. She actually looked happy at the moment. At least, far more relaxed than he had seen her so far.

Totally relaxed, he decided, on his next circuit. At peace.

Utterly unlike the dynamic woman he'd met in that emergency department only yesterday.

It wasn't just the way she was sitting—like a young girl instead of an eminent consultant. He'd seen a totally new side to Jane tonight. Who would have thought they could have so much in common? That they both got so much pleasure from the same kind of books and music, food and wine?

Dr Jekyll and Miss Hyde.

Dylan felt his lips twitch into a half-smile. That might be going a bit far, but he did seem to be discovering two very different people here, and one of them had distinct possibilities when it came to being Sophie's mother.

But which one was the real Jane Walters?

Sophie was finally limp in his arms. A boneless little bundle with her head the heaviest part and one arm extended sideways so it hung in the air. He carried her carefully upstairs and tucked her into the bassinette. Unaware of the faintly determined frown creasing his forehead, Dylan then made his way to the kitchen to get himself another glass of wine before joining Jane on that comfortable-looking couch.

'Is she asleep, then?'

'Aye.' The tone of relief in Jane's voice was annoying, with its inference that the problem was now out of sight and could therefore be put out of mind. He had to remind himself that there seemed to be a better side to this woman. One that might need coaxing to show itself enough for him to be able to test its trustworthiness.

'This is nice,' he said, settling back and stretching his legs towards the fire.

'Mmm.'

'Everything about this place is wonderful,' Dylan continued. He flicked a smile in Jane's direction. 'So different from…'

She pounced on his hesitation. 'From my apartment, you mean?'

Dylan's heart sank at the sharp edge to her words. But what was the point of any of this if he was going to be less than honest?

'Yes,' he said simply.

Jane was silent for a long moment. Then she gave a slow nod. 'Yes,' she agreed. 'It is.'

'You love it, though, don't you?'

'Yes.'

Dylan was encouraged. 'It's a real home.'

Jane's glance was unreadable. As level as her tone. 'It used to be.'

'Did you ever live here?'

'Only on holidays.'

'That's right. You said you had a nanny. And went to boarding school.' Such a different upbringing from his own. It was hard to think there might have been any positive aspects to it. 'How old were you when you started boarding school?'

'Five.'

Dylan's shock must have shown on his face.

'It wasn't so bad,' Jane said calmly. 'I got the best education and a holiday with Gran was always something to look forward to. I loved coming here.'

'How often do you come now?'

'Not often.' Jane gave a soft sigh. 'Too often, maybe.'

She was staring at the fire again. Dylan was staring at her.

'That's a strange thing to say,' he said eventually. 'Why wouldn't you want to spend as much time as you could in a place you love so much?'

Jane caught her lower lip between her teeth, clearly indecisive. She looked up to find Dylan watching her intently, and for a heartbeat, and then two and three, she seemed to reach into him. He kept the eye contact but stayed very, very still.

It was like coming across a frightened deer in a forest, he thought. He had to stay very still otherwise she would turn and flee, and he wanted her to stay so he could watch a little longer.

Whatever she was searching for in his gaze she seemed to find, because she spoke again. In a quiet voice.

A very soft voice.

'As you said yourself, Dylan, it's very different here. It doesn't fit with what I do. Who I am.'

He could taste his disappointment. Like a bitter aftertaste from the wine. The real Jane wasn't the one he would choose as Sophie's mother, then. Or was it?

'Are you sure?' he asked carefully. 'You're certainly a different person here, Jane, but I've learned to trust my instincts and they're trying to tell me that the woman you are here *is* the real you.'

He could hope, couldn't he?

But Jane shook her head. 'I admit that it's part of me. Everyone needs to be able to relax and let their hair down once in a while.' She gave a huff of laughter and raked her fingers through the honey-coloured waves that caught tiny flickers of firelight and gleamed as she pushed it back.

Something deep inside Dylan tied itself into a knot as he watched.

She was beautiful. Remote but very lovely.

'I'm content here,' Jane went on, so quietly she might have been talking to herself. 'And contentment is like chocolate. It's not bad for you as long as you don't have too much at a time.'

Dylan hadn't taken his eyes off her. 'You *ration* happiness?'

Jane seemed startled by his astonishment. 'Too much makes you fat and lazy,' she told him firmly. 'And why do you equate contentment with happiness? Why not achievement? Success? Being the best you can be at what you choose to do with your life?'

Dylan was frowning again. He could feel his forehead creasing as he thought about her words. The tone she had used. Was Jane an 'all or nothing' type of person? How could he ever persuade her that Sophie could be a part of her life if that was the case?

'How much time did you get with your parents?' he asked curiously. 'I've heard about boarding school and the nanny and your folks not being there at prizegivings and sports days or even birthday parties. How often *did* they spend time with you?'

'Not often enough.' He could hear the tension behind those words. See it in the furrow that appeared between her eyes. 'And when they did, something would interrupt it. I learned to wait for whatever was more important to show up, and it always did. A phone call. A hospital visit. An overseas trip.'

Dylan held her gaze. He could see an echo of

the child Jane had been in her eyes. A lonely child who had learned to distrust contentment. To believe it was only to be trusted if you could control the dose. To ration it.

How incredibly sad.

He wanted to take the adult Jane into his arms in order to comfort that hidden child.

Her next words, however, dispelled that urge.

'That's why I'm not going to try and be any kind of a parent for Sophie,' Jane said. 'I made my choice a long time ago and I chose a career.'

The silence hung heavily between them.

'I'm sorry,' Jane said into the silence.

She didn't sound sorry.

'I feel bad that I'm not in a position to take responsibility for Sophie but that's just the way it is.'

Her voice had lost that softness. Dylan could imagine her speaking exactly like this to one of her junior staff members.

I'm sorry you're having to work late but this patient needs to go back to Theatre. That's just the way it is.

Dylan said nothing. He didn't trust that his disappointment wouldn't morph into anger.

'I'll help financially, of course,' Jane continued brightly. 'There's absolutely no problem there. You won't need to work.'

That did it.

'Maybe I want to work,' Dylan snapped. 'Maybe my job is as important to me as yours is to you.'

She hadn't expected that. Her jaw sagged.

'Surprising, isn't it?' Dylan didn't bother to disguise his contempt. 'I'm just a nurse and I have the nerve to think my job is as important as *yours*.'

Jane's jaw snapped back into action. 'Don't you dare make this some kind of personal attack. A platform for whatever reverse snobbery issues you obviously have. We're talking about Sophie. What's best for *her*.'

'Precisely. And seeing as we both feel our careers are so damned important, maybe we should just put her up for adoption.'

She flinched as though he had hit her. 'You can't do that!'

'Why not?'

'She's your niece.'

'She's your *daughter*,' Dylan shot back.

Another silence fell. A shocked one this time.

Jane couldn't believe that Dylan had just said what he'd said.

Give Sophie up for adoption?

Never to see her—or Dylan—again?

She had money, she reminded herself desperately. More money than she could ever need for herself, thanks to her occupation and more than one inheritance. She could make life so comfortable for both Dylan and Sophie. She could have kept in touch and visited sometimes. Been a kind of aunty.

The plan had begun to formulate when she'd listened to him singing as he'd walked the baby to sleep in the kitchen. It had taken more form when he'd talked about how much he loved this place.

She'd even been thinking he could live *here*. In the cottage. With Sophie.

Far enough away.

Close enough.

But she wasn't going to be able to use her financial resources to solve this dilemma. Dylan wanted something else from her.

Something she couldn't give.

'I didn't choose to have a child,' she said finally. Her words wobbled. 'Izzy did. And…and Izzy's dead…' Her lips trembled now. It was a matter of when, not if, she cried.

'Aye.' The anger had gone from Dylan's voice. His face softened, too. Eyes darkened with sympathy. 'I'm sorry you lost your friend.'

'She was more than a friend. She was like a…a sister.'

'Family. I know.' Dylan's eyes looked brighter. Surely not with tears? 'I lost my brother,' he said, with a catch in his voice that made something inside Jane tear apart. 'But I loved them both.'

'So…so did I.' And Jane burst into tears.

The grief was so raw, so overwhelming, that Jane wasn't aware of the precise moment that Dylan took her into his arms. Racking sobs made her whole body shudder. If she'd been alone, she might have curled up into the smallest ball she could and held on to her knees to try and hold back this sensation of being ripped into pieces.

She didn't need to do that because she was being held by arms much stronger than her own.

Held.

Rocked.

And when her own sobs finally ebbed and she could focus on what was in front of her, she pulled back far enough to see Dylan's face and she saw that it was as wet as her own. Dark lashes were still clumped with his tears.

He'd been crying and she hadn't even noticed.

He was grieving as much as she was. Possibly more, and she'd taken *his* comfort without even thinking to offer any in return.

In that moment, Jane hated herself. She had never felt this miserable in her life.

Without thinking, she reached up and wiped Dylan's face with her fingers. 'I'm sorry,' she whispered. 'I'm so sorry.'

He smiled at her.

He actually *smiled*. And then he bent his head and kissed her. Gently. Comfortingly. On her forehead.

And then, as she tipped her face up in a kind of wonder, he kissed her again.

On her lips.

The softest touch. One that sealed a connection. A bond formed by a grief they both shared.

'It's all right, hinny,' he murmured. 'We're in this together and it'll be all right. We'll work something out, I promise.'

'You...you won't let Sophie be adopted?'

'*We* won't,' Dylan corrected her. He shifted a little, which made Jane realise how closely she was still pressed against him. She could feel the hard lines of his chest. Feel the steady beat of his heart. Embarrassed, she sat up, but Dylan was smiling again.

'Thank you,' he said softly.

Jane was mystified. What had she done other than to refuse to be what he wanted her to be?

'What for?' she had to ask.

'For being you,' was all Dylan would say.

What had he meant? Jane wondered as she climbed the stairs to her bedroom later. After they had shared more wine and many memories of Izzy and Josh that had made them both laugh and cry.

He thought she was a different person here. He thought that something she'd always seen as weakness was a more important part of her identity than what she'd spent her life trying to achieve.

She should be offended. Disappointed that she was so misunderstood. Angry that he wasn't hearing what she was trying to tell him. But she wasn't any of those things.

She was exhausted. Confused by such an overwhelming disruption to her life and drained by grief. And in the wake of such turbulent emotions she was now left with a curious sense of peace.

And an emotional talisman in the form of a remembered gentle kiss.

CHAPTER SEVEN

THE memory of that kiss wouldn't go away.

Not that Jane was attributing any significance to what had been purely a gesture of comfort. She wasn't even thinking about it.

It was just…*there*.

As though it had imprinted itself at a cellular level in her body and made an infinitesimal change that was permanent.

A change that seemed to manifest itself in thoughts that were quite out of character.

Like now, when she was well into a careful repair of a baby's cleft lip and palate.

Eyes might be the windows to the soul, she found herself thinking, but lips were a close second when it came to revealing a personality.

You could tell a lot about someone by the way they moved their lips to talk and smile.

By the way they felt when they touched someone else's lips.

This little girl would want to kiss someone one day and Jane was part of a large team of specialists who intended to ensure that the scarring from this birth defect was as minimal as possible. She had an oral surgeon working with her at present. A paediatric dentist had already been consulted, along with an ENT specialist, psychologist, nutritionist and speech therapist.

The goal of this surgery was to separate the oral and nasal cavities and involved drawing tissue from either side of the mouth to rebuild the palate. A plastic surgeon was due to join the team shortly to work on the infant's lips. More surgery might well be needed but what was done today would affect the way the face grew and therefore how well the child might cope socially in years to come, and so it was crucial to get it right.

Not that she wouldn't have been doing the best job she could for this baby anyway, but the errant thought of how important lips were seemed to have raised the stakes.

The facial surgery was only one of several elective procedures on the schedule for Jane's theatre time today and in a specialty such as this, it was a given that timetables would be interrupted by emergencies. Children could get sick and deteriorate so quickly and accidents happened.

The first call to the emergency department came as the cleft lip and palate surgery was finishing. Jane left Mike to supervise transfer of the baby to Recovery. Careful monitoring was essential because of the possible complications that could affect the airway.

The paediatrician who had summoned her to Emergency was Colin Johnston, a fairly new addition to the hospital staff.

'Acute abdomen in a sixteen-month-old boy, Harry Peters,' he told Jane. 'My registrar's been thorough and we've ruled out any intrathoracic infection and UTI. White cell count is unremarkable and the ultrasound is borderline.'

'Temperature?'

'He's pyrexic. Thirty-eight point four.'

'Presenting symptoms?'

'Periumbilical pain, fever and diarrhoea. Pain's not well localised, which isn't surprising.'

'No. You wouldn't expect it to be at this age.' Jane smiled at Harry's anxious parents as they entered the cubicle. His mother was holding the miserable, red-faced toddler, who had obviously been crying for some time.

'Pain relief on board?' she asked Colin.

The paediatrician nodded. 'Morphine. Titrated doses of 0.5 mils. He's a lot happier than he was.'

Jane introduced herself to the parents and the mother's lips trembled.

'He...doesn't really need surgery, does he?'

'If it is appendicitis, yes,' Jane said gently. 'We wouldn't want the appendix to burst because Harry would get a generalised abdominal infection then and he would be a lot sicker.' She touched the baby's head, both for reassurance and to feel his skin. 'Hey, Harry,' she said softly. 'Poor wee man, you're not feeling too good at the moment, are you?'

'Can't antibiotics fix it?' Harry's father asked. 'Without having to operate on him?'

'Not fast enough to prevent rupture.' Jane was checking the outward appearance of her potential patient. He was hot and red but he didn't look dehydrated, which was good. He had almost stopped crying, which was even better. Jane smiled when she found him watching her. Cute little boy. No dimple on his nose, though. Why had she been so confident that it was such an ordinary baby feature? Wishful thinking?

Harry's father was still sounding unhappy. 'I have to say he seems far too young for this. I've never heard of anyone having their appendix out at this age.'

'The youngest documented case was a baby of six weeks.' Jane raised her gaze to Harry's father. 'We're certainly not about to whisk him off to Theatre unless we're very sure it's necessary. I'm going to examine him now and then we'll be watching him very carefully over the next few hours.'

The baby's distress at being examined again increased the parents' anxiety and Jane made a mental note to try and get back to the department herself rather than send Mike for the next evaluation.

'There's a risk, isn't there?' Harry's father was very pale now. His arm was around his wife, who was holding their son again. Tears trickled down her cheeks. A small, frightened family.

'There's a small risk with any surgical procedure,' Jane had to confirm. 'But there's also a risk with the peritonitis that can come from a ruptured appendix. Let's wait and see for the moment. We're going to make Harry as comfortable as possible and watch him carefully. Please, try not to worry too much. He's in the best possible place and we're going to take the best possible care of him.'

Colin accompanied Jane as she headed back upstairs.

'Thanks for that, Jane,' he said. 'I hope the parents aren't going to be scared off signing a consent if it comes to surgery.'

Jane shook her head. 'They want what's best for Harry. They just need to be kept fully informed and involved in the process. I'll get back down in an hour or so, I hope, Colin, but page me if you need to before then.'

'I will.' Her colleague's smile was warm as he turned on the landing to push open the fire-stop doors that would take him in the direction of the wards.

The brush of air from the doors closing followed Jane up the next flight of stairs. She had every confidence that Colin's diagnosis was correct and that he would be managing the case appropriately. So far, she had been impressed with the new arrival to the paediatric team. So impressed, in fact, she had been enjoying the process of getting acquainted a little more than usual.

Colin had proved himself to be competent, methodical and reliable. Traits she approved of. And he was perfectly presentable. Jane also approved of the neatly creased pin-striped trousers he favoured and the crisp white shirt with the brightly coloured bow-ties that she knew his young patients would love. Colin was not only competent and presentable. He was eligible, and Jane had been anticipating a social invitation that would allow them to get to know each other more.

Last week the prospect had been interesting.

Today, as Jane pushed open the doors on the next level to make her way to Recovery and check on her last patient, she realised that any interest had completely evaporated.

Why?

Because Colin's hair was as neatly groomed as the rest of him?

Because his lips were just a little too thin?

And why on earth had she even noticed his lips?

It was ludicrous that Dr Jane Walters, currently being swept along by the kind of professional pressure she loved, could spare even the briefest consideration for someone's lips.

To wonder what they might feel like, touching hers.

To know, with absolute certainty, that they would feel nothing like Dylan's.

And to know, with equal certainty, it wouldn't be good enough.

It was a relief to be able to turn to an entirely clinical line of thought. Happy that the little girl with her repaired cleft lip and palate was doing well, Jane turned her attention to her next case, but the correction of a pyloric stenosis had to be delayed when Jane was called to the paediatric intensive care unit where a neonate had just been resuscitated.

'Sorry about this, Jane,' Colin apologised. 'I was in the ward when this little chap ran into trouble.'

Tiny Liam was only two days old and his abdomen was distended.

'He's been reluctant to feed,' Colin informed Jane. 'No meconium passed and he's running a fever. His collapse was preceded by a spell of vomiting and diarrhoea.'

'Normal pregnancy and delivery?'

'Yes.'

'Mum's not diabetic?'

'No.'

'Let's take a look.'

They worked together for a full physical examination, ordering the laboratory tests and imaging that would be required prior to surgery.

'Shouldn't take long,' Colin warned. 'Can you fit him in later this morning if we confirm Hirschsprung's disease?'

'Of course. Page me.'

Jane sped down to the emergency department then to check on Harry and find there was no change apart from his parents looking a little happier as they got used to their surroundings and the careful monitoring of their son's condition.

Scrubbing up for her delayed scheduled procedure, Jane alerted Mike to the likelihood of the new case in the intensive care unit.

'Congenital aganglionic megacolon,' she elaborated.

'Hirschsprung's.' Mike nodded. 'An ileostomy, then?'

'Yes. I'd prefer to postpone resection of the aganglionic segment until Liam's about six months old.'

'And there's an appendix on the line in Emergency?'

'Yes. Could be a long day.'

'Just the way I like them.' Mike grinned.

Jane returned the smile. 'Me, too.'

And she did. It wasn't just that she had no desire to rush home to her apartment and the odd, empty feel it seemed to have to it since she'd returned from Akaroa. This was her career. Her life. The kind of happiness she had always dreamed of.

Colin had the results from Liam's imaging ready for her as soon as she stripped off her gloves from the delayed case. He even brought them to her in Recovery to save her the time it would have taken for another visit to the ICU.

'I'll go and check on Harry, too,' he offered. 'Shall I get Liam sent in now?'

'Please. I'll grab a coffee and a muffin. Doesn't look like I'll get a lunch break.'

'I'll have to make that up to you.' The smile was a promise. 'I know a superb spot. Your next day off, perhaps?'

'Perhaps.' But Jane's smile felt forced.

She wouldn't be in town on her next day off, would she? She had to return to Akaroa to check on the welfare of her guests. She'd promised to stay for the entire weekend.

What would they be doing right now? she wondered as she entered the small staffroom attached to the theatre suite. Maybe Sophie was lying in her basket under the shade of the old apple tree. Dylan might be digging in the garden or pruning some of those shrubs.

For a moment Jane could almost smell the sea air and the scent of spring flowers. Hear the call of bell birds. Feel the warmth of the sunshine and see the gleam of perspiration of Dylan's arms.

The artificially lit, windowless space of the staffroom suddenly felt claustrophobic.

Jane had never felt trapped in here before. It was disturbing.

Annoying.

Possibly because she now had an obligation to head out of town at the first opportunity and therefore couldn't accept Colin's invitation to what would undoubtedly be a very nice lunch.

Or maybe it was because she wanted to head out of town and had lost any interest at all in Colin Johnston.

Jane ate a rather dry muffin and drank bad coffee, pretending to browse the front page of today's paper to avoid conversation with other staff members. She could feel their presence around her, though. Nurses and technicians. Her anaesthetist. Various registrars and other surgeons. Crowding a space she had never seen as so confining.

Imagine if they could see the mental picture she was having trouble dismissing. Of Dylan with his hair in damp curls on his neck and the muscles in his arms gleaming like that little gold stud in his ear. If they could feel the way that kiss insisted on lingering in the back of her mind. If they knew of the urge she had to ring the cottage, which had less to do with making sure there were no problems than simply the desire to hear the sound of Dylan's voice.

They'd smirk, wouldn't they? And whisper amongst themselves. Jane Walters finding a male nurse attractive? It would be like…like Lady Chatterley and her gardener? Jane might not have that kind of social prejudice herself but she was well aware that it still existed. That the medical hierarchy might, in fact, be one of its last bastions. Dylan would be seen as so far beneath her on the professional ladder that he could be considered a 'bit of rough'.

A bad boy, even.

Bad for her, that was certain. She had earned the respect of the people she worked with and she had no intention of losing it. Finding Dylan attractive was bad enough. Acting on that attraction was as unthinkable as announcing the arrival of an unexpected child.

But there was no getting away from the fact that he was attractive. Jane bit back a wry smile as she pushed herself up from the table only minutes after sitting down.

Izzy would have found all this very amusing. Of course she was attracted, her friend would have declared. It's every woman's fantasy, the bad boy. Independent and a bit wild. Motorbikes and leather jackets.

Jane emptied the dregs of her coffee down the sink. Dylan had a leather jacket. He'd been wearing it the first time she'd seen him. Boots, too. She'd imagined the guitar. It wouldn't have been a very big leap to have it slung across his back as he sat astride a powerful motorbike.

Funny how this room now seemed stifling as well as claustrophobic. It was time to get out of here. Time to centre herself by concentrating on the rest of what promised to be an exceptionally busy—*rewarding*—day at work.

'Do I what?' The question had been startling.

'Ride a motorbike.' The voice on the other end of the line sounded faintly embarrassed.

'I used to,' Dylan admitted. 'A Ducati. Why?' He found himself grinning. 'Do you fancy a ride on one?'

'Good heavens, no!' Jane sounded shocked now. 'No, I was just…um…wondering, that's all.' Her voice became much crisper in the wake of the jarring sound of a throat being decisively cleared. 'I was thinking that you'll need a vehicle while you're here and…'

'And you reckoned I looked like a man who'd be riding off into the sunset on a bike? With my guitar on my back, maybe?'

'Actually, I was simply trying to be considerate, which led me to wonder what you might prefer to drive.'

Dylan's smile faded. He was being put in his place, wasn't he? Kind of a shame to give up on the image of riding a bike again—with Jane clinging on the back. His lips twitched again. They'd probably end up arguing about just who was going to be the pillion passenger.

'I'd prefer something with four wheels and some walls at the moment. With room for a baby seat.'

He hadn't meant to sound resigned but the pleasure of driving Jane's little sports car wasn't going to be on the agenda any more than feeling the wind in his hair on the back of a bike.

Why on earth had Jane even been thinking about bikes? Mind you, knowing that she'd been thinking of him at all was quite nice. The perfunctory conversations they'd had so far this week hadn't suggested that he and Sophie were any more than an obligation.

The usual queries regarding their welfare had long since been dealt with on this occasion but Dylan was enjoying the verbal company. He had no intention of letting Dr Walters escape back to her journal reading or scalpel polishing or whatever she amused herself with before retiring for the night.

'The garden's taking shape,' he told her with

satisfaction. 'I got a path clear all the way down to that shed thing today.'

'The gazebo?'

'That's the hexagonal one with all the roses growing over it?'

'Yes. Lovely place to sit in summer.'

'It will be,' he promised. 'Be a bit painful to try and go inside at the moment. No, I meant the one that's got a kind of yard attached. There's some rusty old netting hanging off poles.'

'Oh! The hen house. Good grief, how could I have forgotten that was there? Collecting the eggs every day was my favourite chore.'

'I could put some new netting up if you want to use it again.'

'Keep hens?' The chuckle told him how ridiculous his suggestion had been. 'I don't think so.'

'No.' But how nice would it be to have a few chooks scratching around at the end of the garden? 'Same goes for the vegetable garden, I suppose?'

'Yes. 'Fraid so.'

There was a short silence. This would be Jane's

cue to end the call. It was Dylan's turn to clear his throat this time.

'There's flowers coming out on the tree at the end of the veranda,' he told her. 'Lots of them. They're bright red and sort of fluffy. I've never seen anything like them.'

'It's a pohutukawa tree,' Jane said. 'It's called the New Zealand Christmas tree because it flowers from now until around Christmas. Gran used to put big bunches in white vases in the house but they drop that fluff everywhere.'

'They're gorgeous.' Encouraged by her enthusiasm, Dylan carried on. 'There's a spruce tree around the side of the house that needs a good trim. I was thinking that a branch would make a perfect wee tree for Sophie's first Christmas.'

There was dead silence on the other end of the line. Was she not expecting him to still be here at the end of December? Or did her lack of interest in the celebration include this part of her life as well as her pristine apartment? He didn't want this conversation to end unhappily so he tried to give her an easy way out.

'But I don't suppose you'd have any decorations.'

She could have just said no and left it at that, but Jane surprised him.

'There's a box somewhere out in the shed,' she said slowly. 'Gran always had a tree. There was a gold star that went on top and when I was little I thought it was the real one, you know? From the story that I never got sick of hearing.'

'The one the wise men saw. I know.'

He let the note of sympathy in his words hang for a moment but he didn't want Jane to dwell on what might be missing from her life. He searched for something positive to say.

'Your delphiniums are looking bonny.'

'What?'

'The delphiniums. Tall flowers. Blue and white. There might even be a pink one in there somewhere.'

'I know what delphiniums are. I'm just surprised that you do.'

'I didn't,' Dylan confessed. 'Marg told me.'

'Marg?' The query was bemused.

'Marg Coates. The lady who lives over the

back fence? Grey hair, early sixties, I guess. She works as a nurse at the local hospital.'

'I don't think I've ever met her.' That hint of annoyance was there again. 'I don't remember her, anyway.'

'She remembers you.' Dylan was smiling again. 'Sweet little girl you were, she said. She often heard you singing and she said you had tea parties for your dolls in that gazebo.'

'That was a very long time ago.'

Her tone made Dylan change his mind about suggesting that Sophie might like to engage in the same activities in years to come.

He could feel the distance between them now. Every mile of those twisting hills and the endless plains. Funny how she'd seemed so close when he'd answered the late call, knowing who it would be. Even closer when she'd shared that memory of Christmas with her grandmother. As though she was actually in the cottage with him. As if he could reach out and touch her again.

He made one last effort to draw her back.

'I think wee Sophie smiled at me today. A real smile and not just wind.'

'She's a bit young.'

'She's six weeks. Marg seemed to think that was the usual time they started.'

'Six weeks already? She'll need vaccinations. Let's see. Six weeks should include diphtheria, polio, tetanus, whooping cough and, I think, hepatitis.'

'She had some of those early, before travelling. I know she's had the hepatitis and polio ones. Not sure what else but it's in with her travel documents.'

'You might like to dig them out. And get her enrolled with the local GP. I think there's a clinic attached to the hospital and it shouldn't be hard to find out who's in charge.'

'Jennifer.' Dylan suppressed the disappointment that Jane wasn't interested in whether Sophie was smiling or not.

'Who?'

'Jennifer Tremaine. Married to Drew Stephenson. They're both doctors and they run the local hospital and general practice.'

'Marg obviously likes to talk.'

'Aye. She does at that. Told me they're desperate for extra nursing staff up there at the moment.'

'Oh?' The word was ominous. 'You're not thinking of applying for a job, are you?'

Oops. How had that happened? They were back to that confrontation of the other night when he'd made that suggestion that they put Sophie up for adoption so they could both continue their lives and careers without compromise.

As if he could ever do that.

He'd only wanted Jane to start thinking. To start feeling involved and it had worked, hadn't it? She'd been jolted into revealing rather a lot about herself.

Her grief for Izzy had been a revelation. Jane Walters was more than capable of caring deeply for another person. That made her quite capable of caring that much for her own daughter.

'No,' he said, after just a heartbeat's hesitation. 'That's not what I came here for.'

It was worth persevering and Dylan intended staying long enough to see this through. For Sophie's sake. Nothing to do with that odd urge to protect Jane that had come when he'd held her in his arms. Or with how incredibly soft he had discovered her lips to be.

Nothing at all.

'You're still planning to come here for the weekend?' he asked quickly.

'Yes. I'll drive over on Friday evening. If I bring you a car, I could catch the shuttle bus back to town.'

'On Sunday.' It was a statement, not a question. It was important that he and Sophie got whatever limited time that Jane could bring herself to take from her job.

'Yes. I'm not on call till the following week-end. We do a one-in-three roster.'

'That's good,' Dylan approved.

'What—the roster?'

'Aye.' He tried to sound convincing. It wouldn't do to let Jane know how delighted he was with the imminent prospect of two days, not to mention two nights, in her company.

For Sophie's sake, he reminded himself as they ended the conversation. The more time Jane had in the company of the baby, the more hope he had of her falling in love with her daughter.

Establishing the kind of bond it would be impossible to break. One that might actually persuade her that a change in the direction of her life might be worthwhile.

For Sophie's sake, he insisted as he flicked off the downstairs lights and made his way up the narrow staircase to his bed.

Yeah…right!

CHAPTER EIGHT

'SHE smiled! At *me*!'

'Of course she did. Told you she's been practising.'

They were all smiling. Sophie was in her bath on the kitchen table again and Jane had just arrived on Friday night. She was still holding her bag in her hand, pausing on her way upstairs to say hello to Dylan, and then Sophie had smiled.

For a moment Jane had been simply astonished. Transfixed by the way the baby's lips curved and then her eyes crinkled as the smile got wider. The bare little body seemed to curl inwards, too, as though she was smiling with everything she had. At *her*! Jane had seen plenty of babies smile but Sophie's was just so gorgeous. A huge, wide-mouth, froggy smile that seemed to stretch from ear to ear and didn't stop.

Jane glanced up at Dylan. Was he seeing this? He was, and he was smiling too so there was no way Jane could help smiling back, and now here they all were with silly, big grins on their faces. The stress of an incredibly busy week simply melted away in that moment in a wash of what felt like…bliss.

'She's getting good at it, isn't she?' Dylan said proudly. He tickled the baby's tummy when the smile finally began to fade and there it was again—this time with a gurgle that was almost laughter and a kick that was hard enough to splash water all over Jane's jacket.

Jane had to blink to try and clear the mistiness that was clouding her vision and her brain. She had to remind herself that all babies looked irresistible when they smiled. Even if Jane hadn't come across another one this week that had that distinctive dimple, Sophie was no different from any other baby she met. She brushed at the water marks that were undoubtedly going to stain the silk of her jacket and excused herself to take her bag upstairs.

It was like kittens, she told herself firmly. Cute as buttons in the pet shop and you wanted nothing more than to take them home, but then they grew up into cats and there they were. A responsibility that had to be fed regularly and taken to the vet and presented an obstacle to getting away if you happened to have a weekend unexpectedly free.

Pets—and children—were for people who hadn't chosen a demanding career. Or for men who had the luxury of a wife who could find fulfilment in creating a home and raising children. Someone that could make the distraction of domesticity a pleasure instead of a necessity.

A female version of Dylan?

The idea of a role-reversal situation was not entirely ludicrous. Jane set her bag on her bed and opened it to remove the clothing and toiletries she had brought with her for the weekend. Dylan would probably embrace the concept of being a house husband. What would it be like, to come home every day to a happy child who smiled at her and a clean house and tidy garden and a meal already prepared?

To an attractive man who would share her life…and her bed?

Oh-h-h… For a moment, Jane simply allowed that tug of desire to ripple through her body. She could almost see Izzy in the corner of her room, giving her a nod and an encouraging smile.

She stripped off her jacket and pulled her hair free of the tight ponytail it was in, running her fingers through the waves to loosen it properly. This was time out, wasn't it? Time to let her hair down and relax. If part of that relaxation was to indulge in the frisson of attraction to a man any woman would fancy, there was absolutely nothing wrong with that. It wasn't as if she was going to let it go any further.

Something like excitement lightened her step as she went back to the kitchen.

'Something smells really good.'

'You hungry?' Dylan had Sophie dried and dressed and tucked into the crook of one arm as he busied himself at the bench.

'Starving. I didn't expect you to cook for me, though.'

'You're not the only one who's hungry. Isn't that right, hinny?' Dylan smiled at the baby he held and then reached to pick up the bottle of formula that was warming in a small jug of hot water. He looked back at Jane. 'I'm doing us some fish. I just put it in the oven so it should be done by the time I've got wee Sophie to bed.' His gaze shifted. First to Sophie, then to the bottle and then back to Jane. 'Would you like to…?'

'Set the table?' Jane interrupted hurriedly. She turned on a bright smile. 'Sure. No problem.' She took hold of the plastic baby bath, grateful for an excuse to look away before seeing any disapproval on Dylan's face. 'Where are you keeping this? In the wash house?'

'Yes…' Dylan sounded as though he was about to say something else but then Sophie whimpered urgently and Jane thought she heard a small sigh. 'It's coming, hinny,' he murmured soothingly. 'Dinna fesh yourself.'

Jane emptied the bath, folded towels and put away the baby shampoo and talcum powder. She could still smell it as she wiped down the table. A nice warm, clean, *baby* sort of smell, which was far from unpleasant and, oddly, didn't seem to clash with the aroma of the food cooking.

The room was warm, both from the oven and the fire that looked to have been burning in the living area for some time before her arrival. Jane found the lighting was soft, having come straight from the clinical glare of hospital spaces, and she could hear Dylan upstairs, moving around.

The cottage felt lived in again. Alive in a way it hadn't been for a very long time. Not since Gran had been here, really, because her mother had kept her town house and only come here for the odd weekend, as Jane now did.

With the table now set, there was nothing for Jane to do but pour a glass of wine and sit and wait for Dylan's return. To relax and enjoy an ambience that was as enjoyable as it was unfamiliar. She never sat in kitchens. Social occasions for her meant restaurants or the dining rooms of colleagues' houses. They certainly didn't include the smell of baby powder or bottles of formula. But this was…nice.

It had been *such* a busy week and, thanks to the disturbance in her personal life, the stress that

Jane normally thrived on had been exhausting. Her life was out of kilter and it was confusing. Why had she felt that simmering resentment at the obligation to come here this weekend when—now she was here—she couldn't imagine a place she would prefer to be?

Dylan said nothing about her avoidance of baby care when he returned to the kitchen. He took a bowl of salad, a bottle of dressing, a pat of butter and a plate of lemon wedges from the fridge, drained potatoes and unwrapped foil packages that came out of the oven to serve what turned out to be the most delicious fish dinner Jane could remember ever tasting.

'This is fantastic. What is it?'

'Cod. Not fancy but it's fresh. Caught this afternoon, in fact. Straight from the sea to your plate, courtesy of John.'

'John?' It was beginning to seem a habit, this echoing of names that meant nothing to Jane.

'John Bellamy. I've met him a couple of times when Sophie and I walk down to the wharf. He's been fishing this harbour for about sixty years, I'd say. Getting on but he's a really nice guy.'

It was silly to feel left out. To resent the notion that Dylan was more at home here than she had ever been. The lemon juice Jane was squeezing onto her fish seemed to be having a sharpening effect on her tone of voice.

'And I suppose he knew my grandmother as well?'

Dylan grinned. 'Probably. But I don't go around talking to *everyone* I meet about you, Jane.'

The resentment faded under the spell of that smile. And Jane liked the way he said her name. It made her feel that she was the focus of his attention. She even liked the inflection that suggested he did talk to some people about her. If he did that, it meant that he'd been thinking about her. As much as she'd been thinking about him, perhaps?

'You certainly seem to have settled in. You must know half the village by now.' Why on earth did that give her an odd thrust of... what...surely not jealousy?

'This is a friendly place and I like to talk to people. It reminds me of home.'

'Really?'

'Especially the wharf.' Dylan nodded as he put

down his fork to take a sip of his wine. 'I grew up in Oban and my dad was a fisherman. My earliest memories are waiting on the wharf for his boat to come in. Being allowed to help with important things. When I was five and I was big enough to lift the rope to go over the mooring post, I was so proud of myself. Josh said if I puffed out my chest any further, I'd pop.'

Jane laughed. 'Did you get to go out on the boat?'

'For a while. We moved to Glasgow a couple of years later and then the only boats we went out on were the ones Dad hired for a week or two on holidays.'

'He gave up fishing?'

'Not by preference. He's got sea water in his veins, rather than blood. He hates the city.'

'So why did you move?'

'It was too hard to try and raise two sons on his own after Mum died.'

'Oh…' He had said his mother had died too young but Jane had let the information slip past and, in any case, it was taking on a whole new significance now. Dylan's brother was dead. So was his mother. That left only himself and his father. Not the ideal combination of family to raise a small girl, was it? Instantly, she was ashamed at the selfish reaction. 'I'm sorry,' she said sincerely. 'It was pneumonia, you said?'

'Aye. She had what she called a "weak chest". Prone to infections. A bit of asthma. It seemed like nothing out of the ordinary except that she got very sick, very fast. Viral pneumonia. She was dead the very next day.'

'And your father brought you up by himself? He didn't remarry?'

'I don't think it's ever occurred to him to replace my mother. She was the love of his life. Josh was older and once we moved and Dad got a job that didn't mean he was away so much, we managed. We had each other.'

A simple statement but it said so much.

The strength of that family bond was almost palpable and Jane couldn't ignore it as she continued to eat.

'Your father must be a remarkable man,' she said into the companionable silence. Willing to sacrifice whatever it took for his family. Like his son.

Dylan had his mouth full and merely nodded agreement. He took another moment to have a mouthful of wine before he spoke again, and his words were unexpected.

'He'd love it here,' Dylan said thoughtfully. 'He didn't want to go back to Oban when he retired. Said he'd feel too lonely by himself, but something new—like this—could give him a new lease of life. With the kind of people here, the hills, the sea. It'd be paradise. Do you realise how lucky you are, Jane?'

'It is a beautiful country, New Zealand,' Jane agreed. 'It's…' Oh, Lord, had she been about to say it's a great place to raise children? '…home,' she amended. 'Sometimes it takes seeing something familiar through someone else's eyes to really appreciate it.'

'True enough.' Dylan's glance was unreadable.

'I cooked,' he said a short time later. 'You get to wash up.'

'Oh?' Jane would have preferred to offer rather than receive an order but she caught the challenge in Dylan's glance. 'Fair enough.'

'And it's your turn to cook tomorrow.'

So much for the image of a domestic god. The fleeting notion that Dylan would embrace being a house husband might have to be crossed off any mental list of future options.

The way she'd been crossed off from serious consideration as a life partner by the men in her life so far? Because she wasn't conventional wife and mother material? What was so wrong with choosing a different direction? Devoting her life to many instead of a select few, with a dedication that was undiluted.

Nothing. It was commendable. Jane was proud of what she did and who she was. She had the right to be defensive if necessary.

'I'll get take-outs,' she said briskly in the kind of tone that her registrars knew not to question.

'Oh? Fair enough.'

The echo of her own response had to be deliberate. So was the tone of faint surprise underlaced with resignation. Dylan stood up, obviously about to leave her alone to her assigned task. It should be annoying that he was challenging her authority. Treating *her* like an underling. It was ridiculous to feel like she had failed some kind of test. That Dylan was disappointed with her.

Jane could feel her cheeks flush. 'Hey, I don't cook,' she told Dylan's back. 'Unless you count scrambled eggs.'

He didn't turn around but she could hear the smile in his voice. 'Consider them counted. Throw in some bacon and I'd be a very happy man.'

It shouldn't matter whether Dylan was a happy man or not. Not this much, anyway. But Jane gathered plates and found herself wondering whether there might be enough fresh parsley growing in the long-abandoned vegetable garden.

Dylan had put some music on and Jane listened as she washed and dried dishes and put them away. It wasn't a record she had heard before but it was beautiful. Classical guitar and a rich, male voice singing a ballad in what sounded like Gaelic.

She stopped in her tracks, stunned, when she finally went to enter the living area and found the music was live. Dylan sat on the piano stool, a guitar cradled as lovingly in his arms as the way he held Sophie, apparently lost in his song.

Jane couldn't move. For a long, long moment, she couldn't even draw in a breath.

That Dylan could make music like this was like…like Sophie smiling. It brought that misty sensation back. A soft, encompassing warmth that was poignant enough to bring the prickle of tears to her eyes.

It made her remember being hugged by Gran. Not that anyone in her family spoke words of love aloud, but that's what the feeling was.

Love.

Was she falling for the gypsy who had brought this music into her life? Along with a baby who had a dimple on her nose and a smile to light up the world around her?

A single, sharp shake of her head was enough to break the spell and enable Jane to move. She wasn't falling for anyone. There was no place for considering that kind of love in her life. Not any more. Not since Gran had died, really.

Not that she'd made any conscious decision to avoid it. God knew, she had tried hard enough to find it again. Tried hard enough to know the heartbreak of being crossed off more than one list of potential mates.

There were things that she was very, very good at and there were things she wasn't. If Dylan got to know her well enough he'd find out, and the truth would be far more disappointing than her inability to cook.

It wasn't going to happen. Jane crossed the room and sat down on the couch. Near the fire but far enough away from the piano stool. The notes of the guitar faded into silence.

'Don't stop,' Jane said lightly. 'It's lovely. Where did you find the guitar?'

'There's a second-hand shop in the village near the supermarket. I couldn't resist it. She's a beauty, isn't she?' Dylan's finger moved over the strings again. 'You sure you don't mind?'

'I'm sure.' Jane curled her legs up and stared into the fire.

She was wrong, she decided only minutes later. She *did* mind. The sound of the music, or possibly more the sound of Dylan's voice, was robbing her of something important. Self-control?

Jane couldn't stop herself watching his hands

as he changed chord positions and plucked the sweet notes from nowhere. Or prevent herself lifting her gaze to watch his lips form the words of the song. And then it lifted again and she found he was watching *her* as he sang.

She couldn't have broken that eye contact if her life had depended on it. And it *felt* like her life depended on it. Desire was so strong, it was painful. She wanted those hands to be touching her body. Creating what she knew would be harmony like none she had ever experienced.

He wanted it too. She could see it in the way his eyes darkened and hear it in the huskiness that crept into his voice.

She was falling into the song.

Falling in love.

And still she couldn't look away.

The huskiness in Dylan's voice became so marked he had to stop to clear his throat. His fingers stilled and Jane could swear she could hear her heart beating in the silence.

Dylan opened his mouth to say something but the words didn't emerge. Instead, Jane heard a thin wail coming from upstairs.

The disappointment was crushing. Dylan held her gaze long enough to let her know he was feeling something similar. His smile was wry enough to suggest how ironic it was that what had brought them together was about to prevent them getting any closer.

'You want to go and answer that?' he asked quietly.

A bucket of cold water couldn't have quenched the flames of desire any more effectively. A flash of panic took its place. Dylan already knew she was a failure with babies. With Sophie in particular. She knew why he wanted her to try again but it wasn't going to be any better this time.

It wasn't that she didn't *want* to help.

She couldn't because she had no idea how to. She would fail. Again. Sophie would be even more miserable and Dylan would be frustrated and disappointed and Jane would feel like an utter failure.

OK. She *didn't* want to help.

Success was what mattered and Jane was old enough to have learned to stay away from experiencing failure. Long-term relationships with men were now well up on that list. So was anything not directly clinical that involved babies.

Jane shook her head. 'No,' she said. 'You'd better go.'

'Morning.'

'Aye.' Dylan's smile was polite. 'It's a bonny one, at that.'

Jane put a mug of coffee down and then sat on the top of the steps that led to the veranda. She nodded in response before taking a bite from the piece of toast she held.

Dylan stayed where he was, in the rocking chair, feeding Sophie. He tried not to notice the low scoop neck of the T-shirt Jane was wearing this morning. He looked away from the soft skin as it rounded into shaping her breasts. But the top was short enough to be leaving a gap at the back as Jane leaned forward, and his gaze skimmed her unblemished lower back, the smoothness only interrupted by the knobs of her spine. What would it feel like to run his fingers over them? Or his tongue?

Damn! If he hadn't got over feeling so attracted to Jane in the time it had taken to soothe Sophie back to sleep last night, he had been certain he'd dismissed the desire when he'd come back downstairs to find that Jane had gone to bed.

Without saying a word.

As though nothing important had happened between them.

And maybe it hadn't. Maybe he'd imagined what he'd thought he'd seen in her face when he was singing to her.

No. Dylan shifted Sophie to his shoulder to rub her back. He knew desire when he saw it. He'd recognised the way his own interest had been fuelled and then ignited into raw need. If Sophie hadn't started crying, he would have put that guitar down, taken Jane by the hand and led her upstairs to her bed.

'The garden's looking wonderful. You're doing a great job, Dylan.'

'Thanks,' Dylan muttered.

Sophie's belch sounded like an echo of his terse response.

He was doing a good job. With her daughter

as well as her garden, but he wasn't here to be her employee, dammit!

'Sophie and I usually go for a walk later,' he said as he stood up. 'You're welcome to come if you want to.'

He had no right to be angry with her.

He couldn't just march into her life and turn it upside down and expect her to be prepared to co-operate. Jane was doing her best here.

She could have stayed back at the cottage and read some of the recent journal publications she had slipped into her bag but, no, here she was, trotting along beside him as he walked with an easy, long stride that had taken them all the way to the lighthouse and out along the jetty and was now going back towards the shops and the beach.

Well, not exactly trotting, but the walk was fast enough to add to this new tension between them and Jane was falling further and further behind. It added to the feeling that she was losing her grip on this situation. A feeling that had become marked enough for her to not want to wait until Dylan came back downstairs last night. She might have lain awake for a long time, struggling with the new complication of how she felt about Sophie's uncle, but she had woken up with a new determination to stay in control. She *had* to!

'What's the rush?' she called. 'We've got plenty of time.'

'Have we?'

Dylan was slightly ahead of her still but he slowed and turned enough to make sure she was catching up. Now she could see Sophie in the front pack he was wearing.

It was quite a picture. The big man with his dark hair tousled by the sea breeze, in his black T-shirt, faded jeans and those cowboy boots with the baby made to look so much smaller nestled against his chest, tiny limbs encased in a pink stretch suit hanging free of the padded support. If he'd been smiling, it would have been an image of idealistic parenthood. But Dylan wasn't smiling.

Jane's concern for his mood must have been apparent in her face. He stopped walking and waited.

'I thought things might have changed,' he said when Jane was close enough to hear his quiet voice. 'That, given a week, you might have got used to the idea and be prepared to at least get to know your wee daughter. You gave the impression that you were interested every time you rang.'

'I was. I *am*,' Jane protested.

People passed the small island they were making on the footpath and glanced at them curiously.

Dylan shook his head. 'You won't feed her. Or change her or even go to her when she's crying.'

'Because she doesn't *like* me,' Jane said defensively. 'You've seen what happens when I hold her. She only cries harder.'

'She doesn't know you. And, at this rate, she's never going to. We don't have that much time, Jane. Decisions have to be made. Sophie needs security. She needs to feel settled. *I* need to feel settled.'

It seemed a strange thing for a man like Dylan to say. Jane raised her eyebrows and waited for him to say more but another couple with a child on a bike were trying to negotiate a way past them and Dylan turned away to start walking again.

The day had started badly and was getting worse. Dylan did have a point. She was avoiding getting too close to Sophie, knowing it would only make things harder. And now she was trying to avoid getting too close to Dylan as well. Shutting herself away in a safe place. Being a coward.

Jane drew in a deep breath and quickened her step as she resolved to make more of an effort.

'Can I buy you a coffee?' she offered. 'My favourite café is just along here.'

It was absurd to feel this pleased to be sitting in the outdoor space of the café a short time later on the white wrought-iron chairs, shaded by the luxuriant grape vines that shrouded the pergola, but Jane was grateful that Dylan seemed to be giving her a chance to try and redeem herself.

It was generous of him. He had been no more prepared for instant parenthood than she had been, had he? He deserved more than her obvious reluctance to get involved.

She was going to try harder. Much harder. She

watched Dylan unclip the straps of the front pack and she swallowed hard.

'Can…can I try holding her?'

Sophie blinked up at her, looking as wary as Jane felt. The soft whimper was out of all proportion to the alarm it generated. Jane looked up, ready to give Dylan an 'I told you so' glance, but his face was screened by the waitress delivering their coffee and the jug of hot water Dylan had requested to warm Sophie's bottle.

He seemed unfazed by Sophie's distress.

'She's just asking for some food, that's all. Here, this is warm enough already.'

The delicious, double-shot skim-milk flat white Jane had ordered sat on the table in front of her, cooling unnoticed, as she nervously attempted to bottle feed an infant for the first time in her life.

'Lay her a bit flatter,' Dylan advised, as Sophie's whimpers threatened to become wails. 'The same position you'd use if she was breastfeeding.'

Jane flushed at the thought. Knowing that Dylan was even imagining the position needed for that tiny mouth to be near her nipple. But he was right. As she shifted the baby's position, Sophie's head instinctively turned, her mouth open to search for sustenance.

She could feel the pressure of the small head on her breast as she slipped the bottle's teat into the gaping mouth. And then Sophie started sucking, staring up at Jane, and that cooling cup of coffee was completely forgotten.

This was…amazing. Holding the warm little body against her heart. Supplying what was needed for comfort and nourishment. Doing something a *mother* would do. Jane could feel that pulling sensation. Like the one that had been pulling her towards Dylan last night, except that it was fundamentally very different. How could something so unrelated to desire be equally powerful? Physical?

That odd tingle in her breasts was sending echoes rippling right through her body. Right up to her brain, to create that misty sensation again. Jane made a valiant attempt to keep control. To make conversation. It wasn't hard to find something to ask because Dylan's strange statement was still on her mind.

'What's the longest time you've ever stayed in one place?' she asked. 'As an adult, I mean.'

Dylan had been watching Sophie intently. His face creased into thoughtful lines before he glanced up.

'A year or so, I guess. Why?'

'What keeps you moving?'

He shrugged. 'There's always new places to see. New people to meet. Maybe you hit the nail on the head. I might have gypsy blood.'

'So you've never been tempted to settle down anywhere?'

'No.' He knew what she was getting at. She could see the comprehension dawn in his eyes. And she could see something more. Respect for the point of view she was formulating? 'I've never found anything that made it seem worthwhile staying in one place.' He paused for a heartbeat. 'Until now.'

His gaze was locked with hers. For one extraordinary moment Jane thought he meant *her*.

He wanted to stay here because of *her*. Not because she was Sophie's genetic mother but because of that unspoken communication between them last night. The physical tingle she was experiencing through feeding Sophie intensified to become a kind of shock wave that made her almost shiver. An electric current that was far from unpleasant.

And then Dylan's gaze dropped and the sensation pooled to become a weight just under her ribs.

'Sophie,' she whispered.

'Aye.' Dylan was intent on the baby again. 'She's stopped drinking, I think. If you give her me, you could drink your coffee before it's stone-cold.'

Jane put the bottle on the table and Dylan stood up. She started to lift the baby to hand her over but Dylan wasn't ready. He was staring past Jane to the table behind her. Swivelling her head, Jane saw a large man who seemed to be having difficulty getting to his feet.

He was pushing the wrought-iron table away to give himself room to move. The table tipped and the man was on his feet but he was hunched forward, with one hand on his throat.

The universal sign for choking.

His face was rapidly turning purple. Jane heard

his female companion gasp in horror but her attention had flicked back to Dylan.

To the change in his expression as he focused on the unfolding emergency. Now he was moving swiftly.

A life was in danger and Dylan McKenzie wasn't hesitating.

CHAPTER NINE

THE choking victim wasn't as tall as Dylan but he was a good deal heavier and on the point of collapse.

Dylan's arms were keeping him on his feet, wrapped around him from behind, his hands joined to form a ball that he was using to try and produce an artificial cough. Pressing in and up just under the man's ribs.

Again and again he demonstrated an excellent Heimlich manoeuvre. Jane sat, frozen, holding Sophie. So grateful that Dylan was here because she wouldn't have had anything like the physical strength needed to do what he was doing.

The man was limp in his arms now, however, and Dylan let him gently down to the paved court-yard, kicking a chair out of the way. He opened the man's mouth and swept a finger inside but clearly couldn't find any part of what was obstructing the airway. Kneeling beside the victim, he positioned his hands on the centre of his chest and gave several compressions, the same way he would have if the man had been in cardiac arrest. Then he grasped a shoulder and hip, pulling the man onto his side, supported against his own body, and gave him what looked like hefty blows with a flat hand on the centre of his back.

Jane held her breath as he rolled him back, checked his mouth and then started the chest compressions again.

'Call an ambulance,' someone was yelling behind her.

'Shane!' The woman who had been sitting at the same table as the man was sobbing. 'Oh, my God! Shane!'

'I saw Dr Tremaine,' someone else shouted. 'She was in the supermarket about ten minutes ago. I'll go and see if she's still there.'

'Yeah…' A man close to Jane was staring at Dylan. 'Does this guy know what he's doing?'

'He's a nurse,' Jane snapped. 'And I'm a

doctor and I can tell you he knows exactly what he's doing.'

Dylan seemed oblivious to the shouting and chaos around him. He was thumping the man's back again, and suddenly there was a convulsive movement. The man gagged, struggled and then coughed up what looked like a large piece of bacon rind.

It had been well under two minutes since Dylan had spotted the emergency. Within another minute the man's colour had returned, he had regained consciousness and struggled to sit up.

'Keep him lying down,' the man who had queried Dylan's ability advised. 'I've done first aid and I know you don't let them move until the ambulance gets here.'

'He needs to breathe,' Dylan said calmly. 'It's much easier to do that if you're sitting up.'

It certainly seemed to help. Supported by Dylan and the man's still white-faced compan-ion, he was dragging in ragged breaths, one hand pressed against his chest.

'You have pain?' Dylan queried.

'Yeah.'

'Do you have any history of heart problems?'

'No.'

'You've been getting pain, though, babe,' the woman said. 'When you went for that run the other day, remember? And when you were mowing the lawn.'

'Was the pain there before you choked?' Dylan asked.

'Yeah…I guess. It was… Real hard to swallow.'

'Why didn't you say something?' the woman cried. 'Oh, *Shane*!'

'I'm OK, Rae. Don't…fuss. I…just need a minute.'

He didn't look OK, Jane thought. His face had taken on a greyish tinge and he was sweating profusely. She would have said something but Dylan's assessment was as good as any she could be doing.

'How does it feel now?' Dylan had his hand on the man's wrist, feeling for a pulse.

'Like…it's hard to breathe… It's sore. Heavy.'

'Just in your chest?'

'No…in my throat…'

'Oh, God!' Rae said. 'Has he still got something stuck in there?'

'I don't think so,' Dylan responded. 'Anywhere else, Shane?'

'My arm.'

'The left one?'

'Yeah.'

'How bad is the pain? On a scale of zero to ten, with ten being the worst you can imagine.'

'It's getting up there. I'd say…ten.'

The group of horrified onlookers parted to allow a dark-haired woman through.

'Hi, there. I'm Jennifer Tremaine. One of the local doctors.'

'Dylan McKenzie. Visiting nurse. This is Shane. He's… How old are you, Shane?'

'Forty-six.'

Dr Tremaine nodded. 'I hear you choked? How's your breathing feel now?'

'Pretty good.'

Jane caught the glance Dr Tremaine gave Dylan. One of respect. Appreciation. Admiration, in fact.

'Good job,' was all she said, with a flash of a smile, before turning back to Shane, but Jane found herself staring at the back of her head. She was a very attractive woman, probably in her early thirties. Single?

No. Dylan said the hospital and general practice were run by a married couple. Not that it was any of her business. The relief she was aware of was undoubtedly due to the fact that Shane now had two medical professionals caring for him so she didn't have to hand Sophie over to some stranger and get involved herself.

She couldn't have handled the situation any better than Dylan. If she was honest, she'd have to admit she couldn't have done as well as he had. The rescue had needed a strength she didn't possess to save the man's life in the first place and now Dylan was giving a handover that let the doctor know there was more to the case than a simple choking.

'Crushing, ten out of ten, central chest pain, radiating to his throat and left arm. No known cardiac history but possibly some previous angina. Pain came on before he choked.'

A four-wheel-drive vehicle with a flashing orange light on its roof had pulled up outside the café.

'This is our local ambulance,' the doctor told Dylan. 'I want to get Shane up to the hospital and get a twelve-lead ECG and some bloods off. We can transport him to town from there. By chopper, if we need to.'

'It's my heart, isn't it?' Shane asked fearfully. 'Am I having a heart attack?'

'Oh, my God!' Rae was sobbing again.

'It's a possibility,' the doctor told him calmly. 'And it's a case of guilty until proven innocent in cases like this. Right now we're going to give you some aspirin, put some sticky dots on your chest and see what's going on, and get you up to the hospital. I can give you something for that pain as well.'

'Thanks. Can Rae come with me?'

'Of course.' The doctor looked up. 'Um… Dylan?'

'Aye?'

'I couldn't ask you to help, could I? My husband's at home with the kids and we're single-crewed on the ambulance. Just with the stretcher and things until we get him to the hospital?'

'Sure.' But Dylan turned away for a moment. 'If it's OK with Jane.'

'Of course.' Jane nodded. 'We'll walk up and meet you there.'

She watched them get Shane onto a stretcher and then into the back of the modified Jeep. She could see Dylan putting the leads of the life pack on Shane's chest and pulling an oxygen mask from its plastic wrapping. The doctor was gathering supplies needed to start an IV line as the ambulance officer helped Rae into the front passenger seat. As he closed the back doors, Jane caught a glimpse of Dylan holding an ampoule up as he drew the contents into a syringe. Presumably morphine for Shane's pain. He looked completely at home in the back of the ambulance. As though he'd been part of the team for a long time.

He fitted in. Yet again Jane was left with the unsettling impression of being an outsider. Not that she'd ever had any ambition to belong to the community in what was only a weekend retreat so why did she feel as if she was missing out? That she was watching something she'd probably like to be a part of but she had no idea of how to join in.

The perspective of looking in from the outside was strengthened when Jane arrived at the hospital about half an hour later. She'd seen the rescue helicopter fly overhead before she was halfway there, largely thanks to the length of time it had taken to figure out how to use the front pack and make sure Sophie was secure. In the end, a waitress had helped and she'd given Jane a curious look.

'You were with the guy that saved that man from choking, weren't you?'

'Yes.'

'I thought you were a family, you know? That this was your baby.'

'N-no. I'm just…helping.'

The little worm of shame at her response had refused to go away. It got bigger once Jane had set off on her journey with Sophie strapped to her chest, nestled between her breasts.

'Sorry, Soph,' she found herself whispering aloud. 'It's not fair, is it? Not knowing where you belong. Who you belong *to*.'

It was a bit embarrassing to receive the indulgent smile of a woman, walking hand in hand with a little girl of about seven or eight, who passed close enough to notice her whispering. Looking down, Jane could only see the top of a downy head but the heaviness of her burden suggested that Sophie had gone to sleep. There was nothing to stop her continuing the conversation silently, however.

Who will you be holding hands with when you're old enough to walk by yourself?

With a new mother? The woman who might be lucky enough to win Dylan's love?

What would they say to Sophie? How would they explain the name on the birth certificate?

There's a woman called Jane Walters, she imagined them explaining. *She lives a long way away, in New Zealand. She gave her egg that could make a baby to her best friend.*

Jane could almost hear a child's clear voice in her head. An older Sophie who had questions.

Why didn't she want a baby?

She's a doctor who has a very busy job. A busy, important job.

That would make Jane no better than her own mother had been. Worse, in fact, because she wasn't even a part of Sophie's life.

Or maybe Sophie would know about 'Aunty Jane'. The woman who lived on the other side of the world and sent birthday cards and presents. Someone for whom regular photographs needed to be taken. They might even tell Sophie the truth.

She did meet you, they might say, *when you were just a wee baby.*

Why didn't she want to keep me, then?

The brutal answer to that would be that she didn't want to be a mother. That her job was too important. And how would that make Sophie feel? Jane knew. God, she knew only too well.

She wasn't aware of the tears in her eyes until she almost missed the turning she needed to take to get to the hospital. Nearly missed her footing completely and tripped on the edge of the footpath.

She could have fallen. On top of the tiny baby she held. Blinking back the tears, Jane stood still, trying to calm herself enough to stop her heart racing and let her take in a breath that wasn't a horrified gasp.

What was she doing? Trying to prove that she wasn't fit to be anyone's mother? Sophie had woken up with the jolt and obviously agreed. The loud cry was a miserable wail by the time Jane entered the wide, panelled hallway that led from the impressive entrance of the old hospital building.

The howls bounced off the walls and echoed down from the high, ornate plaster ceiling. The peace and quiet was being shattered and Jane felt mortified. There could be seriously unwell patients in the rooms that opened off this hallway.

The woman who appeared in a nurse's uniform was smiling, however.

'That must be wee Sophie I can hear,' the woman said. 'We've been expecting her. And Jane…how are you, my dear?'

'Um…fine…' The woman looked familiar enough for Jane to hazard a guess. 'Marg?'

'Goodness, how long is it since I've seen you?' The older woman's face creased. 'Your mum's funeral, it would have been.' She stepped closer to peer over the back of the front pack. 'What's up, little one? You don't sound too happy.'

'She's been fed recently,' Jane said. 'I don't think she's hungry.'

'What about her nappy? When was she last changed?'

'Ah…I'm not sure.' Dylan would have attended to that before they'd set out for their walk, but that was hours ago now. 'Not for a while.'

'That'll be what the problem is,' Marg said confidently. 'Have you got another nappy?'

'Oh…no!' Jane bit her lip. She was doing a good job of making herself look totally inadequate here. 'I left the bag at the café.'

'I'm not surprised.' Marg smiled. 'You had a fair distraction going on there from what I've heard. We've got plenty here, in any case, over in the maternity suite. Would you like me to take Sophie and sort it out?'

'Oh, I couldn't ask—'

'It would be a pleasure.' Marg was already helping her with the clips. 'We're not busy and a baby is such a treat.'

A very elderly lady appeared at the door of the room closest to where Jane was removing the front pack. She was gripping the handles of a walking frame with difficulty and peering very short-sightedly into the hallway. Her voice was quiet and as shaky as her hands.

'I thought I could hear a baby.'

'It's a precious little girl, Enid. Would you like a peek?'

A face that was already a mass of crinkles folded into a smile. Marg looked at Jane. 'Is it all right if I show her off? It would bring a lot of joy to more than one of our oldies.'

'That's fine. I know you'll take good care of her.'

'We certainly will.' Marg kissed the top of Sophie's head. 'We'll get you a clean bottom before we do anything else, though, won't we, pet?'

Jane smiled her appreciation but her glance was drawn to another figure appearing slowly from a room further down the corridor.

'That's Tom,' Margaret said. 'He'll want to know what's going on and I have to say it's the first time he's made the effort to get out of his chair for a week.'

'That's good.' But Jane was looking past Tom.

'If you keep walking that way, you'll find Dylan and Jenny. She's just giving him a quick guided tour of the treatment rooms and so forth.'

Jane nodded a greeting to both Enid and Tom and kept going. She passed more rooms. Comfortable rooms with French doors opening onto a shady veranda. Pictures hung on walls beside oxygen and suction outlets and flowers were arranged in old china vases. No doubt the Christmas decorations would come out within the next week or so, with tinsel and paper bells and a tree that had real gifts underneath. It felt relaxed and homely and not at all like the medical facilities Jane was used to.

The treatment areas were more familiar. Modern additions to the original building that were sleekly functional and very well equipped. She found the attractive young doctor and Dylan in animated conversation.

'X-ray facilities and a theatre for minor ops,' Dylan was saying as she got closer. 'You're very well set up for a ten-bed country hospital.'

'It seemed a shame to let Drew's talents go to waste.' Jennifer Tremaine was smiling. 'As it would be with yours. I—' She broke off as she noticed Jane's approach.

'Hi,' she said warmly. 'It's a pleasure to meet you, Dr Walters.'

'Please, call me Jane.'

'And I'm Jennifer. I met your mother a few years back, when she first got sick.'

'I remember. You managed her treatment and transfer very efficiently. I read your notes. I'm sorry I didn't come and thank you in person.'

'No problem.' Jennifer grinned. 'You can make up for it by persuading Dylan to come and work for us. We're so short-staffed at the moment, it's not funny.'

'It's a bonny wee hospital,' Dylan put in. But he was frowning. 'What have you done with Sophie?'

'Sophie?' Jennifer sounded surprised.

There was a tiny pause. A hesitation on Dylan's part that let Jane know he expected her to answer the query.

'The baby,' Jane said, before the pause got really awkward. 'My…'

No. She couldn't do it. To say it out loud was to claim the relationship. She couldn't do that.

She couldn't live up to what that relationship entailed and the damage of not doing it well enough was too huge. She couldn't let Sophie grow up knowing that kind of hurt.

'Dylan's niece,' she amended smoothly.

'You have a niece that's travelling with you?' Jennifer's eyes widened. 'How old is she?'

'Six weeks.'

'Oh! And her parents? Are they visiting as well?'

'No,' Dylan said quietly. 'Sadly, her parents were both killed in an accident recently.'

'Oh...I'm so sorry.' Jennifer was also very curious. She glanced from Dylan to Jane and back again, pressing her lips together, obviously restraining herself from asking for more information.

Dylan took pity on her. 'Jane was a close friend of my brother's wife,' he explained. 'I wanted to break the news in person.'

'And you came all the way from Scotland with a baby to do that? Wow!'

The tone was one of amazement, heavily laced with admiration. Dylan was becoming even more a hero and he didn't appear to be in any hurry to jump off the pedestal.

He simply smiled. And that smile was directed at Jennifer.

'How's Shane?' Jane's tone was clipped. '*Was* he having an MI?'

'He certainly was,' Jennifer nodded. 'Massive ST elevation on all inferior leads. We gave him oxygen, morphine and aspirin and sent for priority transport. You probably heard the helicopter?'

'Yes. Very efficient.'

'We would have started thrombolysis if there'd been any delay but he should be in the catheter laboratory within an hour from onset of symptoms and angioplasty is the best option.' Jennifer smiled at Dylan. 'Yet another reason I need to persuade you to come and work here. Not many of my nursing staff are experienced with monitoring a patient that *does* require something like a streptokinase infusion.'

'I'm only here on a visitor's permit.'

'You could upgrade,' Jennifer suggested eagerly. 'With a working permit you'd get at least twelve months in the country, I think. Probably longer, if you have an employer prepared to sponsor you.'

Jane couldn't decide whether the possibility

was good or not. Twelve months. A whole year to get to know Sophie.

And Dylan.

But what then? They'd be so much a part of her life nothing would ever be the same.

'I couldn't anyway,' Dylan said apologetically. 'As tempting as it is, I've got this wee bairn I'm looking after.'

'I could guarantee any number of people who would be more than happy to help in that quarter, but it's up to you, Dylan.' Jennifer glanced at her watch. 'I'd better go. Drew will be wondering why on earth I'm not home with the supplies for lunch.'

She walked both Dylan and Jane back towards the main entrance, pressing a buzzer on the reception desk.

'That'll bring Marg back,' she said. 'And your wee Sophie.'

She paused on her way out the main doors. 'Think about it,' she said to Dylan. 'And call in if you have any questions. Better still, come up for dinner some time soon. We're in the phone book. Bring Sophie.'

* * *

He was thinking about it for the rest of the day.

How could anyone not fall in love with a charming country hospital set on a hill with a view of that stunning harbour and the surrounding hills?

With patients who were comfortable and well cared for by people who knew them personally? While a lot of the nursing care would be routine, the links with the community as a whole would make up for that, wouldn't they?

And there'd be emergencies. Like the one today. Trauma cases as well as medical ones that would need stabilising before they could be transferred to the larger hospital in the city. Babies would be born in that lovely new maternity wing. Children probably came in to recuperate after surgery elsewhere. There would be enough variety in any case to keep the job interesting.

Jane didn't seem particularly enthusiastic about any of it. She seemed to be avoiding him for the rest of the day. Reading journals and dead-heading roses in the garden and making a trip to the supermarket for groceries. To her credit, she did produce the scrambled eggs and bacon for their dinner and Dylan tried to make an effort as well. To start a conversation that was more than polite and monosyllabic.

'Jennifer's lovely, isn't she?' he asked.

'Mmm.' Jane was busy buttering a slice of the fresh bread she had served to accompany their simple meal. 'She certainly seems to be happy as a GP here.'

'Her husband was a specialist surgeon in the States for years.'

'Really? And he came to work *here*?'

Dylan ignored the implied put-down. 'It's because of him they've got the X-ray facilities now. And the theatre. They can do more than small stuff if they have to.'

'How on earth did they meet? Was he here on holiday?'

'I don't know.' What was it about Jane's tone that made him feel defensive of a small town he'd only been living in for a week? 'I'll ask her when I go for dinner, shall I?'

Jane gave him a look that provoked something like rebellion.

She didn't like the idea of him working at the hospital. Why?

Because she thought it was his job to make sure Sophie was cared for and nothing else should matter to him?

Because she didn't want him around for that long?

That wasn't the impression Dylan had been given last night. In those magical few minutes with the flicker of firelight and the soft notes of his music and Jane looking at him like…like…

Dylan sighed. It was a given that he would have led Jane upstairs to make love to her if Sophie hadn't interrupted that moment, but he wouldn't have even considered it if he hadn't been damned sure that Jane would have been as willing as he was.

She had wanted him but she had thought better of it. Because Sophie had reminded her of her presence? Was the reason Jane didn't want him here for a long time because it meant that Sophie would also be here?

His *niece*.

She hadn't even had the decency to acknowledge the relationship *she* had with this tiny, vulnerable human being.

It wasn't good enough.

Maybe it was time to stop being nice. Making excuses for Dr Walters.

Dylan met Jane's glare steadily. 'You really don't want me to stay here long enough to make it worthwhile getting even a part-time job, do you?'

'You wouldn't want to stay here that long anyway,' she countered swiftly. 'You never have before so why start now?'

'I told you,' Dylan said patiently. 'Sophie needs to be settled. To have a place to call home and grow up in. The way I see it, I could do a lot worse than settle in a place like this.'

'But…why *here*?' Jane had put her fork down, her appetite apparently deserting her. Her hand was resting on the paper serviette lying beside her plate. Dylan watched with interest as her hand closed into a fist, trapping the serviette. He could hear the edge in her tone that sounded like panic. He looked up only to catch her avoiding eye contact, but if she thought she was hiding by doing so, she was wrong. Dylan was watching her very carefully.

'Why not?'

'What about…your family? Your father?' Triumph was winning over any panic now. 'He won't want to miss seeing his only grandchild growing up.'

'True,' Dylan conceded calmly. 'So it's just as well he'll love being here, then, isn't it? He'll love the harbour and the boats and…' He couldn't help a quick smile. 'And it's the perfect answer to getting help with wee Sophie while I go to work.'

Jane shook her head. 'Have you any idea how difficult it is to emigrate these days? You might get a working permit but your father isn't likely to qualify. And what do you do after the twelve months or two years or whatever? Pack *every-body* up and move on somewhere else?'

Dylan said nothing. He was too busy watching. First the way the serviette was being scrunched and torn and then the way emotions were flitting across Jane's features. It was hard to analyse what was going on behind eyes that were far more brown than green at the moment. So dark. Distressed.

Was that was she was afraid of? That she would get attached to Sophie and then he would take her away somewhere else?

'Why…*here*?' Jane repeated. The query was a pale, puzzled echo of the previous demand.

Dylan reached across the table and put his hand over the fist that was clenched around the ball of soft paper.

'Because you're here,' he said softly. 'Because you're wee Sophie's mother.'

To his amazement, Jane's eyes filled with tears.

'I'm not a mother,' she whispered. 'I don't know how to be.'

'You'll learn,' Dylan promised. 'I can help.'

'But—'

'It doesn't have to happen overnight. We can have all the time we could possibly need if I settle here.'

'But…' Jane was staring at his hand, which was still covering hers. She seemed mesmerised by the way he was stroking his thumb over her skin. Slowly. Firmly enough to, hopefully, convey reassurance. 'It won't be easy,' she continued. 'You might not be allowed to stay.'

'Oh, I think we could get around that.'

'How?' Jane looked up and… Yes, that flash in her eyes couldn't be anything other than hope, Dylan was sure of it.

He smiled. 'You could marry me, hinny.'

CHAPTER TEN

'*MARRY* you!'

'Aye.' Dylan's mouth twisted into a wry, lopsided smile. 'Is the prospect *that* horrible?'

'It's—it's preposterous!' Jane snatched her hand away from his touch.

Eyebrows rose as the corners of his mouth fell, making him look absurdly disappointed. 'Why?'

Jane gave an exasperated huff. 'We barely know each other.'

'I think we're getting to know each other very well.' Dylan's gaze was softening. Very intent. Reminiscent of the way he'd been looking at her last night over the top of his guitar. That look of connection.

Of desire.

Jane's heart gave a painful thump and then

started racing. Her mouth had gone so dry she instinctively licked her lips and then saw the heat that darkened Dylan's eyes into that extraordinary dark blue and her heart missed another beat. What woman alive wouldn't fall for someone like this?

He was the most gorgeous man she had ever been this close to. Physically beautiful with those expressive eyes and lips and that tousled dark hair. Big and strong and—the glint of gold in his ear caught her eye—a little bit wild. He was also intelligent, capable of using his strength when it was needed but also capable of being astonishingly gentle. She had seen him use that gentleness with Sophie. With his music...

This was crazy. She was actually excited by the notion of marrying him?

'You're crazy,' she whispered.

His head shake was slow. Sure. He got up from his seat on the other side of the table and came to her side. He pulled out the chair beside her and perched on its edge. He took hold of her hand again and this time Jane didn't pull away. She couldn't. She was too stunned, both by his suggestion and her reaction.

'I'm Sophie's uncle,' Dylan said quietly. 'The closest thing she's ever going to have to a real father.'

Jane couldn't refute the statement so she kept listening. She concentrated on the sound of his voice to try and distract herself from the way it felt to have him holding her hand.

'You're her mother,' Dylan continued. He gave her hand a little squeeze, then, and she felt that squeeze run up her arm and then spread through her whole body. 'Or as close as she's ever going to have. Don't you think it's only right that her parents should be married to each other?'

'Not…not if it's being done for the wrong reasons.'

'Is giving wee Sophie a wonderful place to grow up and a whole family around her so very wrong?'

'N-no.' Of course it wasn't. Jane's brain was curiously foggy. There was a reason why it was completely wrong, she just couldn't catch hold of it.

'We don't have to live in your gran's house, if that's what's bothering you. I have plenty of money. I can buy another house. Two, even. One for me and Sophie and one for her grandpa. We passed a wee house that had a "for sale" sign on it today. Not very far away from here at all.'

Jane shook her head. 'An obvious marriage of convenience for the sake of giving someone residency would get you sent out of the country like a flash. They check up on discrepancies like that.'

Dylan's smile held more than a hint of satisfaction. 'So we'll have to live in the same house, then. But not with my da.' His smile was fond. 'Not that he's not a lovely man, mind, but it might be just a wee bit stressful for you to live with an extended family when you've been used to being on your own. Too much to ask from a newlywed.'

'I'm not… I *can't* marry you!'

But if she didn't, Dylan would go away and take Sophie with him. Maybe not immediately, but eventually he would have to leave the country. Jane could feel an odd ache now. As though her arms were aware of something missing. Were they remembering how it had felt to hold Sophie this morning while she fed her? Yes. That ache was located inside her chest. Near her heart. Just where Sophie's tiny head had been resting.

'Would…?' Her throat was so tight, Jane had to pull in a new breath to release her words. 'Would it be a marriage in name only, then?'

Dylan still had hold of her hand. He was also holding the eye contact but he said nothing.

A second ticked past. And then another.

And then, without breaking the eye contact, Dylan leaned forward. Close. And then even closer.

Jane could feel his breath on her face. The warmth of his skin. She could see every one of his incredibly long, dark eyelashes. She had to close her eyes as she felt him move again. Felt his head tilt and his lips touch hers. A feather-light touch. Across her top lip and then her bottom lip.

Oh Lord, was she sitting here with her eyes closed and her mouth open like a stunned mullet?

Jane's eyes snapped open to find Dylan had drawn far enough away to be watching her. So intently, he seemed to be looking right into her soul.

She closed her mouth and then licked lips that

felt curiously abandoned seeing as he hadn't actually kissed her. Or had he? Desire was spiralling out of any hope of control. Jane could feel a pulse hammering in her neck. Her limbs felt oddly weak and heat was pooling in her belly.

Yet it hadn't been a kiss. Not a *real* kiss.

Jane couldn't look away. Couldn't think. Her whole body was clamouring for a real kiss and not just that experimental touch.

This time, when Dylan closed the gap between them, she was ready. It might even have been her movement that closed the gap. The touch was just as gentle but it was on both her lips at the same time.

And then Dylan's fingers slid into her hair to cup the back of her head and the pressure of the kiss increased. A tiny sound like a moan came from somewhere deep within Jane and was lost inside Dylan's mouth.

She was lost inside that mouth.

Mirroring his action, Jane slid her fingers into the tousled curls on his head, revelling in the luxuriant, thick waves as she tried to anchor herself as the kiss came alive.

Tantalisingly, he broke the contact of their lips again, drawing back to stare into her eyes, his own dark and unsmiling. And then it was Dylan's turn to make a sound. A raw sound of…what…defeat? Surrender? Whatever it was, it gave Jane a sense of power that she had never experienced before. He wanted *her*. More than any man had ever wanted her.

This time the kiss was nothing like any gentle exploration. The pressure was bruising. Their tongues tangled. Dylan's hands moved to grip her shoulders and then slide down to brush exquisitely tender nipples and mould breasts that felt swollen with desire.

When they finally had to draw apart to take a breath, they stared at each other again in a kind of wonder. The only sound was their ragged breathing.

And then, amazingly, Dylan smiled.

'No,' he said hoarsely. 'I dinna think this will be a marriage in name only, do you, hinny?'

Jane couldn't catch her breath enough to form a coherent word so she did the only thing her body would allow her to do. She shook her head.

'The wee one's asleep,' Dylan whispered. 'Do you think that…?' He touched her lips with his. Softly. Unbearably softly. 'Maybe…' He kissed her again. Slowly. 'We should give this marriage idea a wee test run?'

Jane gulped in some air. She was watching Dylan's mouth. Waiting for it to come close enough to claim with her own. Her lips were trembling with anticipation.

'Y-yes.' She had to force the word out because she wanted to do things with her lips that had nothing to do with talking. 'I…think we should.'

'Aye.' Somehow, Dylan managed to stand up, scooping Jane into his arms as he did so. And he managed to carry her up the narrow staircase and into her bedroom. He put her down on the edge of her bed, kissing her again until she felt so boneless she leaned back and Dylan let her go until she was lying across the bed.

'Don't go away,' he said softly. 'I'll be right back.'

It took a moment or two for Jane's brain to start functioning. To stop feeling bereft and wonder what Dylan was doing. Had he gone to check on Sophie? Find a condom?

Jane was shocked that she wouldn't have thought of either of those necessities. Even now, applauding him for his ability to think beyond what was happening between them, she was aware of disappointment.

Dylan wasn't as carried away by passion as she was. Yes, he wanted her. Possibly as much as she wanted him, but he wasn't lost in it.

He wasn't in love with her.

This wasn't about her. It was about testing the possibility that a marriage of convenience might be enough to be satisfying for both of them.

No. All of them.

Because this was for Sophie's sake, wasn't it?

Was it enough of a reason? Jane sat up, pushing back hair that felt as tangled as her emotions. She could pull the plug on this. It might be incredibly difficult but it would be possible. She could avoid getting any deeper into a chain of events that was changing her life irreparably.

But then Dylan came back into her room. He

pushed the door almost closed. Giving them the illusion of privacy but leaving enough of a gap to hear a baby cry.

He had taken off his T-shirt and his chest was bare. The way it had been that first morning, in her apartment. When Jane had been disturbingly aware of what she now recognised as the stirring of an attraction that was far too powerful to resist.

And, as if that wasn't enough, Dylan was smiling. That amazing smile that made her feel so special.

So safe.

'Now,' he said, so softly his words caressed her skin, 'where were we?'

This was the real Jane Walters.

A very beautiful woman who was far more vulnerable than she would ever want to admit.

He'd seen right into her soul in the last twenty-four hours. That look on her face last night when Sophie had smiled at her!

At *me*, she'd said. As though nobody ever gave a smile purely due to the delight of seeing her.

And this morning, when she'd been holding Sophie and feeding her, he'd seen the softness. The ability to love.

Tonight he'd felt it himself. Had felt it and tasted it and buried himself in it, and he knew that nobody would ever be able to give him what Jane was capable of giving him.

But he had to tread carefully. To treat winning her heart with the same care he might use to coax a wild deer to come closer. The way he had encouraged her to talk to him last week. Jane was vulnerable because she needed something in her life she'd never had enough of so she'd never learned to trust it. Instead, she'd learned to shut it out. To convince herself she didn't want it.

It was something Dylan could give her enough of.

Love.

He kissed her again now, as tenderly as he knew how to, and she gave a soft sigh in her sleep and curled more closely against him. Skin to skin. As they had been for many hours now.

Who would have thought that Dr Walters—the ice queen—eminent specialist in complete control of her career and lifestyle could be capable of such passion?

Of responding to even a whisper of a touch but just as easily matching the greedy movements of an almost desperate need?

She was perfect.

Was he being unfair, trapping her into marriage like this? No. He had to drive this forward. If he allowed her too much time to think and consider the implications, she might take fright at what could lie ahead and decide it was safer to remove herself from his life entirely.

He couldn't allow that to happen.

He'd come here to find Sophie's genetic mother. He might have found something entirely unexpected in Jane, but Dylan knew with absolute certainty it was something he was never likely to find again. It was unique. Precious. Definitely worth fighting for.

Jane was afraid because she didn't think she could make a success of this new challenge life had presented. She didn't know how because she'd never been set any kind of example, except maybe from her grandmother whom she'd only seen for holidays. That made any kind of family a temporary thing. Something to visit but not a part of daily life. The most important part.

Dylan could change that. He could show her what it really meant to be part of a family. To love and be loved. They would all benefit from that. He would. And so would Sophie and Jane. Maybe Jane most of all. She deserved to. It was because of Jane that Sophie existed at all, and while it hadn't been intentional and perhaps Dylan wouldn't have considered settling down and raising a family any more than Jane had, Sophie was already the most precious thing he'd ever had in his life.

Jane was rapidly moving close to being the second most precious thing and, if they could build on what had happened this weekend, it was highly likely that the two females now in his life would hold a place of equal importance in his heart.

Not that he could let Jane know that.

He could show it, maybe, by loving her with his body the way he had last night, but Dylan knew instinctively that to speak any words of love would have doors slammed in his face.

Jane had been hurt before. Too many times to count, probably, by her parents' lack of interest. She hadn't found any man she was prepared to commit to, either. It was too soon to hope that she could trust anything he might say. He needed more time. *They* needed more time.

What better way to ensure they got all the time they could possibly need than by making this a permanent arrangement? It was inspired.

Sophie woke up as the first light began to chase darkness from beneath the eaves of the cottage. Instead of making the interested cooing sounds with which she had begun to greet a new day, her cry demanded instant attention.

With a sigh, and a soft kiss on Jane's bare shoulder, Dylan eased himself from the bed and went to tend to the baby.

Jane came down to the kitchen a little while later. She frowned at Sophie.

'She doesn't sound very happy.'

'No.' Dylan jiggled the howling bundle in his arms. 'She didn't seem very interested in her breakfast, either.' He watched Jane as she held the kettle under the tap to fill it with water. 'How 'bout *you*, hinny?' he asked in a brief lull between the wails. 'Are you happy?'

The glance he received acknowledged their night together. Her smile let him know he had made her very happy. But she looked tired and the frown hadn't gone away. She looked as though her thoughts were occupied by more than the steps it would take to make coffee.

'The shuttle leaves at 10 a.m.,' she told Dylan, raising her voice so she could be heard over Sophie. 'I'll get sorted after breakfast and get you to drop me at the bus stop if that's OK.'

'Why don't I drive you back to the city?' he suggested. 'I could come back again this afternoon and a drive might be just the ticket to get this wee lassie settled.'

The baby was still fretful by the time Jane was ready to leave, and she found herself sympathising with Sophie's low-level misery.

She was feeling a bit like that herself.

Like she didn't want to go back to the city. To her job and apartment and reality because Dylan didn't belong in that reality.

All the reasons why a relationship with

someone like him would undermine the esteem with which her colleagues regarded her would be obvious again. She couldn't hope to keep the proposed marriage a secret any more than the astounding news of her instant motherhood, and Jane dreaded the exposure.

She dreaded the notion of losing Dylan and Sophie even more, however. Maybe Dylan McKenzie, male nurse and ex-gypsy, was nothing like what she would have considered as husband material, but the last two days had shown her he was everything she could possibly have wished for. She hadn't known what she wanted—*needed*—until it had arrived in her life.

There were still a frightening number of problems but the best thing seemed to be to tackle them one by one.

The first problem appeared before they'd even left the cottage.

'Do you think she feels hot?' Dylan asked.

Jane threw her bag into the back of the vehicle and then moved to reach into the back seat and put her hand on Sophie's forehead.

'She's warm, certainly, but I don't think she's running a temperature.'

'She's very red.'

'She's been crying on and off for quite a while. Did she have any of that last bottle?'

'Aye. Maybe half of it.' But Dylan didn't look happy.

'She's well covered up and it's not a cold day. Why don't you take some layers off while I lock up? I'll drive, if you like, so you can keep an eye on her.'

The rumble of the engine and the movement of the car soothed Sophie to sleep not long after they left the township. Dylan gave an occasional anxious glance over his shoulder to the car seat in the back, but finally seemed to relax.

Jane wished she could.

'Do you really think we could make this marriage idea work?' she asked finally, as they toiled through the bends of the steepest hill.

'We'll find a way.'

'How?' Jane had been trying unsuccessfully to think of a solution to the most pressing issue. 'I can't give up my work.'

'I wouldn't expect you to. Your job is an important part of who you are, Jane.'

It was all she'd been until Dylan and Sophie had changed her life. Had it only been just over a week ago? So much had changed. Way too much to go back and have things the same as they were. A week ago that was all Jane might have wished for and now it was the last thing she wanted.

'You do want to settle here.'

'Aye.'

'In Akaroa, I mean.'

'Aye. I meant that too.'

'You'd be happy, wouldn't you? Working in that little hospital and living in that small cottage?'

'Aye.'

Jane sighed, changing gear to negotiate a particularly sharp bend on their way downhill. 'I work in the city, Dylan. In a big hospital that has a specialised paediatric department. Commuting for ninety minutes, twice a day, on a road like this, is not an option.'

'You can come at the weekends, yes?'

They would be leaving the hills behind them

soon. Getting closer to the city. Jane could feel reality reaching out with a chilling touch.

'I do a ward round most Saturday mornings. I'm on call every third weekend. Actually, I'm on call *all* the time, because I've made it clear that I want to be contacted if any of my patients are in trouble.'

Dylan said nothing.

'If I'm only visiting occasionally, it'll cause the same problems that would happen if you were living in a separate house. Eventually, the immigration authorities would become aware of it. They'd be quite within their rights to say that it was simply a marriage of convenience for the sake of you gaining residency.'

'But Sophie would be all right, yes? As your daughter, she's automatically a citizen of New Zealand, isn't she?'

'She was born in the UK.' Jane shook her head with a sigh. 'It's a legal minefield. I suppose it'll be all right as there are no other parties laying any claim to the right of raising Sophie but even so, I think I should contact my solicitor this week. What if, a couple of years down the track, you get sent home and they don't allow you to take Sophie out of the country? What then?'

'I wouldn't go,' Dylan said calmly. 'End of story.'

'They could make you.'

'There's no point in creating problems that aren't there yet, Jane.'

They might not be there yet but they weren't far away.

Dylan and Sophie would have to live in the city. In her apartment? Hardly. Jane would have to factor in house-hunting to her schedule, along with a wedding and, presumably, immigration arrangements for Dylan's father.

The house would need some kind of a garden. Proximity to a school. They'd be able to go to the cottage for some weekends, of course, but would that be enough for Dylan, when he'd fallen in love with Akaroa as a place to live and its miniature hospital as a place to work?

Thoughts tumbled and whirled. Jane hardly noticed the frequency with which Dylan was turning to check on their small passenger in the back seat. Until…

'Pull over!' The instruction was terse.

'Why?' Jane flicked him a glance but Dylan was staring into the back of the vehicle.

'Just do it. *Now!*'

Jane put her foot on the brake and indicated that she was pulling off the road. An angry toot from a following car told her she hadn't been clear enough about her intended action but Dylan's tone had an undercurrent she had heard often enough in her medical career.

Controlled fear.

The tyres skidded a little in the loose gravel on the side of the road and then bumped over grass. Jane brought the vehicle to a standstill, took it out of gear and turned off the ignition.

Dylan was halfway out of the car by the time she'd pulled on the handbrake. He was wrenching open the back door to reach Sophie as Jane turned her head.

'Oh, my God!' she whispered.

The baby was jerking uncontrollably. Her eyes were half-open and rolled back so that only the whites were showing. Worse still, her lips were turning a nasty shade of blue.

Jane fumbled with the catch of her seat belt.

Dylan had unhooked the car seat by the time she got out. He was undoing the safety belt that held Sophie in the seat as she arrived on his side.

'She's burning up!'

'It's most likely to be a febrile seizure,' Jane said, touching Sophie's skin. 'Take her stretch suit off. I've got a bottle of water. We'll sponge her. We need some paracetamol. Or ibuprofen.'

'Isn't she a bit young for a febrile seizure?' Dylan's fingers were struggling with the snap fasteners on the front of Sophie's little pink suit— a task he normally managed with surprising ease.

'Here, I'll do that.' Jane slipped her hands beneath his. 'Normal age range is three to eighteen months but it seems the most likely cause. Unless...' Jane pulled the small limbs from inside the stretch suit. 'She hasn't been stung by anything, has she? A bee or something?'

'Anaphylaxis?' Dylan's face was so pale it looked like he hadn't shaved this morning. 'No. I'm sure I would have noticed. She hasn't been in the garden today.'

'She's breathing again,' Jane noted in relief.

'Her colour's getting better. Get the water, Dylan. The bottle's in the compartment between the front seats.'

The convulsion had stopped completely by the time Jane had peeled off Sophie's singlet. No sign of a rash that could indicate they might be dealing with meningitis, thank goodness. Her breathing seemed fine and the awful blue tinge had gone from her mouth. Jane strapped her back in her seat.

'What are you doing?' Dylan demanded.

'We have to get her to hospital,' Jane snapped. 'You can sponge her while we get going.'

A minute later they were on the road again. Dylan was in the back seat beside Sophie, sponging her gently with a wad of tissues he dampened with the drink bottle. He was ready to keep her airway open if she had another seizure.

Jane gripped the steering-wheel so hard her fingers hurt.

She had her foot flat to the floor, ignoring the speed limit on the long, straight stretches when it was safe to do so. If she got chased by traffic police, she would just tell them this was an emergency. That they didn't have time to wait for an ambulance.

It was no use telling herself what she would tell any other parent in this situation. That febrile convulsions were scary but quite common and almost always harmless. What if this wasn't simply due to a high fever? What if it was something like encephalitis? The result of birth trauma she knew nothing about? Or a brain tumour? Or something else that would put Sophie's life in danger?

Sophie.

Her daughter!

CHAPTER ELEVEN

'SOPHIE *WALTERS*?' The emergency department consultant flicked Jane a sharp glance.

'My daughter,' Jane said.

Dylan was aware of something changing. He could feel it, inside his chest, as he stood by the bed holding Sophie, in the resuscitation area they'd been rushed into. The dreadful fear that was consuming him was still there, but Jane's words were having a curious effect. As though she'd thrown a verbal net over his fear. Giving it a limit.

She had claimed her daughter.

She might seem in control here, in the familiar environment in which he'd first seen her, but she was as white as a sheet and her eyes showed the same kind of fear that Dylan was experiencing.

'She's just had the single seizure?'

'Yes.'

'How long did it last?'

'Less than five minutes.'

'Put her down on the bed,' the consultant instructed Dylan. 'Let's get a temperature, stat,' he directed the nurse, who had just spread a clean sheet onto the bed.

Dylan caught Jane's gaze as he laid Sophie on the bed. He couldn't smile but he could try and give her what she had just given him.

An ally.

They were in this together. As Sophie's parents.

The nurse gently fitted the earpiece of the tympanic thermometer into Sophie's tiny shell of an ear. Dylan held her steady.

'It's all right, hinny,' he said softly. 'You're safe.'

'Temperature's 40.3,' the nurse reported.

'Breath sounds are equal. Chest's clear.' The consultant lifted the disc of his stethoscope from Sophie's chest. 'Can we get that nappy off, too, please? I'd like to check her skin properly.'

Another doctor entered the room.

'Ah, Liz,' the consultant greeted her. 'Just the

person.' He turned to Jane. 'You'll remember Liz? She would have still been in the paediatric surgical department when you started here.'

Jane nodded. 'You went to the States, yes?'

The red-headed woman, probably in her late thirties, returned the nod. 'And I see you've followed my example and become a mother?'

'Um…yes.'

Liz raised an eyebrow but her attention was already too focused on Sophie to query the hesitant response.

'Normal pregnancy and birth?'

'As far as I know.'

'Yes,' Dylan put in.

'You're Sophie's father?'

'No. I'm her uncle. But I heard a lot about the pregnancy and birth.'

Liz exchanged a glance with the consultant and then looked back at Jane. 'Is Sophie adopted?'

'Not exactly. Genetically, she's my daughter.'

'Surrogacy?'

'Kind of.'

Liz gave up for the moment, busy examining Sophie who was crying miserably. 'Has she been unwell in the last few days?'

'Only this morning,' Dylan responded. 'She seemed out of sorts. Off her food and crying more than usual.'

'Running a fever?'

'She felt warm, but nothing like she does now.'

'Let's weigh her, please,' Liz said to the nurse. 'And we'll get some ibuprofen on board. Ten milligrams per kilogram of weight.'

When the nurse had administered the liquid medication by slipping a small syringe into Sophie's mouth, Liz shone a torch into the baby's eyes and then turned her to check the skin on her back.

'No sign of any rash developing.'

'Thank God for that,' Dylan murmured. Watching Sophie having to undergo a lumbar puncture to exclude meningitis would be unbearable.

'No vomiting or diarrhoea today?'

'No.'

'I'm going to have a look in her ears,' Liz told them. 'Can one of you hold her, please?'

Dylan looked at Jane. Jane looked back and they held the eye contact for a heartbeat.

'I'll do it,' Jane said.

She wrapped Sophie in a light cotton blanket and then cradled her against her chest, one hand over the back of her head to hold her still as Liz put the earpiece of the otoscope carefully into place and then peered in to view the eardrums on each side.

Sophie hated it. She wriggled and howled and Dylan saw Jane biting her lip and blinking as though she was close to tears herself. But finally the examination was over.

'Definitely otitis media,' Liz announced. 'Nasty red drums in there. I'm happy enough that the infection is responsible for both the high temperature and the seizure.'

Jane was still holding Sophie. Rocking her gently by twisting her own body from side to side. Sophie was hiccuping and snuffling but the loud cries were fading.

'You don't think a full blood count is necessary?'

'Not when there's an obvious infection going on.'

'What about an MRI or EEG?'

Liz shook her head, smiling at Jane. 'You're

thinking like a parent, not a doctor. We'll keep a close eye on her for a few hours but I'm confident it was a febrile event. She's looking happier already, with the anti-inflammatory kicking in, don't you think?'

Jane looked down. Sophie's eyes were half-closed and one tiny fist was gripping a finger of her hand. She had stopped crying. There was a kind of wonder in Jane's eyes as she looked up at Dylan. This time he could find a smile, no problem.

'We'll start antibiotics,' Liz said. 'And I'm going to drag you off to the staffroom and find some coffee for you, Jane, as soon as I get a break. I'm dying to hear all about how this baby has come into your life.'

'So Liz was a paediatric surgeon? Like you?'

'Yes. A very good one. She took up an amazing position in a children's hospital in Washington, DC, and met her husband over there. They had their first baby three years ago and another one last year and decided they wanted to come back to New Zealand to raise their family.'

'Why is she working in the emergency department?'

'The hours suit her and she preferred it to
going into general practice. Her husband also
works a little less than a full week and they have
a nanny to fill in the gaps.'

Dylan looked up from where he was giving
Sophie her bottle of formula. From the cubicle
they'd been moved to for observation, it was
possible to see a large portion of a department that
was surprisingly busy for a Sunday afternoon.

'It's a good place to work, Emergency,' he said
thoughtfully.

'You want a job here?' Jane moved her head
to look at Dylan more closely but she didn't
move her hand. She was sitting on the chair
beside Dylan and Sophie was gripping her
finger. Squeezing it at frequent intervals that co-
incided with a renewed sucking effort. She was
making up for a hungry morning.

'No.' Dylan's tone was decided. 'I'd much
prefer the cottage hospital in Akaroa, with a bit
of everything from minor surgery to obstetrics.
You'd never get bored with that and it has the

added bonus of a small staff. You'd get to know everybody so well.'

Jane let go of the hope that Dylan might want to work and therefore live in the city, which might make planning their future a little less complicated.

'No,' he said again. 'I was thinking *you* might like to.'

'*Me?*' Jane's jaw dropped. 'I don't think so.'

Dylan didn't meet her gaze. 'Just an idea,' he said mildly. 'Liz obviously enjoys it and part-time work would give you more time with... with Sophie.'

Why the hesitation? Jane wondered. Had he been going to say 'with us'? No. The whole reason for her to be with Dylan was Sophie, wasn't it?

It was time to change the subject. Before she relayed the information that Liz wasn't that happy with her current employment. And that during her conversation with Jane she had come up with the extraordinary idea that they could share a single surgical position and both be doing the job they loved with enough time to be with their children as well.

Jane had dismissed the notion with vague references to how difficult it would be to persuade management to accept such an unusual arrangement. She'd also said she had no plans to sabotage her career to such a degree, but she hadn't told Liz everything. She hadn't mentioned the proposed marriage or how she felt about her daughter's uncle, and that probably had far more to do with her negative reaction than the challenge of making the idea a possibility.

Downsizing her job would be an astonishing sacrifice and, if she made it, she would be committing that much more of her heart and soul to this strange little family she'd been given. To a man who wasn't prepared to consider living in the city for *her* sake.

He didn't feel the same way she did. This was all for Sophie's sake and Jane had to remember that because otherwise she might start hoping for something she couldn't have. She'd end up as she had been as a child. Trying to please. Desperate for a sign that she was loved for herself. Getting hurt, time after time.

Giving away half her career was the adult equivalent of that trying to please. To win love. Jane wasn't going to allow herself to do that. Not for Dylan. Not even for Sophie.

She was already making major changes to her life for them. She had agreed to marry Dylan, for heaven's sake, to give him the security of knowing he could stay in the place he wanted Sophie to be raised. By doing so, she was sacrificing any chance of finding a man who would fall in love with her the way she had with…

Dylan.

The name was a silent sigh, wrenched from her heart.

A surrender.

There wouldn't be another man, in any case, because Dylan was so different. Unique.

Amazing.

Jane had to make an effort to distract herself before she did something embarrassing, like starting to cry. She had to focus on the most important person involved in all this. Not herself. Not Dylan. Certainly not herself and Dylan.

'She's looking so much better since her temperature started dropping.'

'Aye. And she's nearly finished this whole bottle.' Dylan smiled down at the baby. 'Oink, oink, you wee piglet!'

The suction on the teat broke with a small ping and sizzling sound. The corners of Sophie's mouth lifted. And kept lifting. She lay there, grinning up at Dylan with a dribble of milk escaping to run down her chin.

Jane lifted Sophie's bib to catch the dribble but she couldn't catch that misty sensation that enveloped her. She recognised it now. She may not have chosen to bring this baby into existence or given birth to her herself, but it *felt* like she had. She loved this child as much as if she had made those choices.

'Will you stay in town tonight?'

'I don't think we need to. Liz said she'd come and do a final check soon but her temperature was almost normal last time and she said if it stays down we can go home.'

'What if she has another seizure? There's a higher chance of a baby who's had one febrile event to have another one.'

'Only if the temperature gets high enough, which it won't if I keep up with her medication doses.'

'She'll need watching.'

'I know that.' Dylan's tone was very patient and Jane bit her lip.

'Sorry. I know you know. And I trust your care of Sophie completely. You're doing an amazing job of looking after her.'

He glanced up and caught her gaze. 'It's nice to know you trust me, hinny.'

The odd endearment and more—that smile—brought back that misty feeling and intensified it to the point that Jane's brain went completely foggy.

She was smiling back, lost in the fog, until his next words brought her back to the present.

'I've got the hospital just up the road, too. And Jennifer, if I need any help.'

'Mmm.' Jane dropped her gaze to Sophie again. The most important person.

'Everything's back at the cottage,' Dylan continued. 'The bassinette and the bath and the formula and nappies. We didn't bring much with us and it's a bit late to try hitting the baby shops.'

'Mmm.' Everything Dylan was saying made perfect sense. Far more sense than the strength of her reluctance to see them go. This kind of separation was something she'd have to get used to if they were going to make this marriage of convenience work.

She could feel Dylan still watching her. Did he think she wanted him to take himself and the baby away to make it easier for her to slip back into her usual routine?

She should want that. Last week she had wanted that, but it was different now. Sophie was sick. She needed…her mother?

It was too big a leap. She wasn't ready for this. For any of it.

Liz came back into the cubicle and spent a few minutes checking Sophie.

'You're a little poppet, aren't you?' The doctor smiled at Jane and then Dylan. 'She's gorgeous. And she's bounced back fast enough for me to be quite happy to let you go home. Her temperature's virtually normal and she's feeding well. Keep up the anti-inflammatory and the antibiotics till the course is finished. Not that I need to tell either of you that. I'm confident you won't have any further problems. Are you both happy with that?'

'Aye,' Dylan said. 'Thank you very much.'

'Yes,' Jane added. 'Thanks, Liz. You've been great.'

As they walked out of the department, Jane had to admit to herself that she hadn't been telling the truth. In a very short space of time she would be watching Dylan and Sophie drive away and walking back to her apartment by herself.

And she wasn't happy with that.

Not at all.

He kissed her, which only made it harder.

Sophie was settled in her car seat. Facing backwards but strapped into the front passenger seat so that Dylan could see and talk to her on the journey.

The driver's door was open. Dylan was ready to get in and drive away but he stopped beside Jane.

'Are you sure you don't want me to drop you home?'

'I'm sure. It's only a short walk and I could do with the fresh air. Drive carefully.'

'I will.'

'Ring me when you get back to the cottage.'

'Aye. I'll do that too.'

He put his finger under Jane's chin to tilt her head gently upwards. Then he bent and covered her lips with his own. A lingering, soft kiss that took her straight back to the night they'd spent together. Only last night but it felt like forever ago.

Dylan broke the kiss but pulled Jane into his arms and held her. Briefly. Firmly enough for her face to be pressed against his shoulder.

'We'll miss you,' he said simply.

Jane drew in a deep breath, inhaling the scent of him. Imprinting the feel of his warmth and strength into every cell of her body. So that she could remember it on the nights ahead when she would be alone in her bed. As if she could have forgotten!

Her words were muffled. It was quite possible that Dylan didn't hear them.

'I'll miss you, too.'

CHAPTER TWELVE

SHE missed everything.

The smell of the sea and the clutter of the cottage. The sound of the birds and Dylan's guitar and Sophie's gurgles. The sight of Dylan's smile. *Sophie's* smile.

She'd be having her bath now, Jane would think while she waited for her frozen microwave meal to heat. Grinning and kicking her legs and making conversation with those interested coos.

Dylan might be listening to music in front of the fire, she would think later, trying unsuccessfully to make sense of the article in the journal she held. Or *making* music. Putting a classical CD on didn't help a bit. It only made the longing worse. It was just as well she had no Cat Stevens in the apartment or she might be a basket case by now.

They would both be asleep, she would decide in the early hours of yet another night. As she should be herself but it was hard, because missing it all was a physical ache that wouldn't go away.

Work should have helped. As busy and rewarding as ever, with an endless supply of new patients and the pleasure of ticking off a successful outcome for recent ones. Like little Harry, who was discharged with a clean bill of health a week after his appendectomy. And tiny Liam, who was now feeding well and gaining weight. Why did every baby remind her of Sophie? And every father of Dylan?

Thoughts of them were always there, a low background hum, the way that first kiss of Dylan's had lingered. It went up several notches when the Christmas decorations went up around the hospital. When the excited gleam came into the eyes of the children and every parent expressed the wish that their sick little ones would be home well before the actual day.

Jane had every sympathy with the parents. Christmas was a time for families to be together. Dylan and Sophie were *her* family now. She had to tell herself that the ache of missing them would become familiar. She'd get used to it. There would always be a weekend to look forward to so the ache would diminish.

Except it didn't.

Sometimes it went away for a while. During a particularly intense session in Theatre, for example. Or during the often lengthy conversations she had by phone with Dylan every evening.

'Sophie's fine,' he told her late in that first week. 'Last dose of antibiotics today and I took her up to the clinic and got Jennifer to check her ears.'

'She's happy, then?'

'Who? Sophie or Jennifer?' Dylan laughed and the sound made Jane smile. She leaned back in her chair, the phone pressed hard against her ear, and closed her eyes for a moment to savour the sound.

'Sophie's very happy,' Dylan continued. 'And so's Jennifer. I've agreed to do an afternoon shift for her. Just one or two a week. Wednesdays and Fridays to begin with. First one tomorrow, actually. From 3 p.m. to 11 p.m.'

'Who's going to look after Sophie?' The delight of hearing Dylan laugh morphed into something much less pleasant. Alarm? No. More like jealousy.

'Ruby,' Dylan said reassuringly. 'Hospital cook and a lovely woman. Mind, she almost came to blows with Marg while they argued about who was going to have the privilege.' There was a tiny silence, as though Dylan became aware of the vibes from Jane's end. 'Are you OK with that, Jane?'

'I'm fine with it,' she said. And realised it was true. She wanted Dylan to be able to do whatever made him happy. Happy and settled and not wanting to go anywhere else. 'Did you make that call to your father last night?'

'Aye.' A new warmth entered his voice. 'He's thrilled to bits. Told me my mum had a book about New Zealand once and used to dream of living here one day. I told him I'd get a digital camera so I can email him pictures of the harbour and the boats.' Dylan chuckled. 'You know what he said?'

'What?'

'"Forget the boats, it's the wee lassie I want tae see."'

Jane laughed. 'I'm looking forward to meeting him. Did you go and look at that house?'

'Aye. It's fine. Small but perfectly formed. I'm going to put an offer in on it tomorrow.'

'That's great.' And it was. Another sign that Dylan was planning to make a permanent home here. With Sophie. With her. It was perfect. Almost.

'You don't want me to leave it until you can see it, too? You know more about houses around here than I do. We could look in the weekend.'

'I'm on call this weekend, remember?'

'Oh… That's right.'

Was it her imagination or did he sound disappointed? And if he was disappointed, was it just because he wanted help in caring for Sophie? Or someone to share his bed?

Having to remember that Dylan probably wasn't missing her in anything like the same way she was missing him suddenly made the ache unbearable.

'It's my job, Dylan. There's nothing I can do about it.'

Her tone was sharper than she had intended, which probably explained the silence she got in response. Jane sighed.

'Put an offer in if you're happy,' she said. 'If you think your dad will be happy. As far as where it is for amenities and so on, I think you have a better feel for the place than I do. You live there now and I just visit.'

'Aye.' The word was heavy enough to be a punctuation mark.

A fitting end to the conversation.

Except that Jane didn't want it to end.

'I saw my solicitor again today. He says that he can start proceedings to ensure that we are both legally considered to be Sophie's parents but—'

'*But?* What's wrong?'

'Nothing. He just said that…um, it would make things less complicated if we were married before the paperwork is done, otherwise there'd be a bunch of amendments that would have to be approved.'

'We'd better get married as soon as possible, then.'

Jane had to swallow the lump in her throat. How often would she have to deal with the reminder that Sophie was the reason this marriage was happening? The only reason.

'I'll look into what needs to be done. I guess you'd want just a registry office?'

'No way!' Dylan's indignation was a surprise. 'I want the real thing here, Jane. In a church, thank you.'

'Yes.' Jane swallowed again. 'It should look real, shouldn't it? I suppose I'd better do something about a dress.'

'Aye. And I'll get my dad to bring over my kilt.'

Jane didn't need to swallow now because her mouth had gone curiously dry at the thought of Dylan wearing a kilt.

Different again.

Special.

'I've never been married before,' Dylan said softly into the silence. 'And I don't intend doing it again. I want this to be real.'

Jane found herself nodding. They had to make it look real, didn't they, so there would be nothing for anyone in the immigration department to get suspicious about later.

They finished the call a short time later but Jane lay awake for a long time that night, thinking about the conversation.

She wanted this marriage to be real, too, but for very different reasons.

Real meant loving each other. Maybe having more children. A real family.

They both loved Sophie. She loved Dylan. Surely that was enough of a start, considering the length of time they had known each other? Was it too much to hope that one day she would earn Dylan's love?

Jane rolled from her side to stare up at the ceiling. If she tried hard enough, she could earn his love.

No. She tossed herself back, pushing her face into her pillow. She'd been there. Done that. It didn't work.

The weekend on call was exceptionally busy and Jane was called to the emergency department more than once to consult on cases that looked like they might need surgery. Because Liz was on duty, she knew that the calls were genuine and Jane was more than happy to respond to every one.

There were babies with potential intestinal obstructions and an unusually high number of trauma patients. A child who had fallen from a tree and another from a bicycle. One had been struck by a car and another had fallen from her pony while jumping at a one-day event. Liz was particularly interested in this twelve-year-old girl, Briar.

'My daughter's desperate to have riding lessons,' she told Jane. 'It's a worry!'

'Is she stable haemodynamically?'

'Yes. Blood pressure remaining within normal limits. She's extremely tender and there's free blood in the abdomen visible on ultrasound.'

'He didn't mean to stand on me,' Briar told Jane. 'And we were coming first, too! We won dressage and went clear in show jumping and— Ooh…my tummy *really* hurts.'

Jane examined the girl gently and reviewed the ultrasound results. She talked to Liz.

'There's a space in CT if you want to send her for a scan.'

Jane nodded. 'Have you spoken to the parents about the possibility of a laparotomy being necessary?'

'Yes. Do you want to talk to them, too?'

'Let's wait and see what the scan shows.'

'I'll get that organised. Have you got time for a coffee before she comes back?'

'I'd love one.'

They had the staffroom to themselves a few minutes later.

'I can't believe how busy this weekend is turning out to be.' Jane sighed.

'Tell me about it,' Liz agreed. 'At least you get the satisfaction of following these kids into Theatre. It's frustrating to know they need surgery and have to hand them over.'

'You really miss Theatre, don't you?'

'Wouldn't you?'

'Yes.' But she wouldn't necessarily miss this, Jane thought as she sipped her coffee. So much time on call when she could be somewhere else. With someone else.

'How would you envisage it working?' she asked tentatively. 'A job-sharing arrangement, that is.'

'Whatever worked for us both,' Liz said promptly. 'Maybe two and a half days a week each? Monday morning till midday on Wednesday? Turn about with weekends on call. Is it still one in three?'

'Yes.'

'So that would be one weekend on in six for each of us. That wouldn't be so bad.'

'No. But what about continuity of patient care?'

'Communication,' Liz said confidently. 'And respect for each other's opinion. I think we'd work well together, Jane.'

How well became apparent when Briar came back from her CT scan with results that showed internal injuries that were potentially serious. One kidney was bruised, her liver lacerated and she had a splenic fracture. It wouldn't have been unreasonable for a surgeon to take her straight to Theatre but Jane and Liz looked at each other. They took a second look at all the images from the scan.

'She's clinically stable,' Liz pointed out.

'And there's good delineation of the extent of the injury on scan.'

'The bleeding might well have stopped already.'

'Let's treat her conservatively, shall we? Keep a close eye on her.'

'Absolutely.'

Jane went to the ward to check on Briar late

that night before she finally headed home and she was back again early the next day. By Monday evening, she was able to ring Liz and tell her they'd been justified in delaying surgery. Briar was showing significant improvement.

'We'll keep her in for another day or two and do another ultrasound.'

'Thanks for letting me know, Jane. And have a think about that job-sharing idea.'

'I will,' Jane promised.

She did.

Jane was still thinking about it on Wednesday when she decided to take the longer route home, through the park. She was tired, thanks to a normal working week on top of the busy weekend, and she thought a walk in the cool air of the early evening might freshen her up and clear her head.

It could work, she mused. She could find the satisfaction she needed from her job, even with vastly reduced hours. She might even find more, because she wouldn't spend so much time being so tired.

Dylan might find it enough to be in Akaroa for only half of each week and he could work whatever shifts he wanted during those days. If he was prepared to compromise to that degree, and if Jane could find a suitable house not far from her hospital, it really just might work.

A house like that one, over the road from the park. An old stone house, almost hidden by ancient oak trees, with a garden that looked out over the river. On impulse, Jane turned left instead of right when she reached the corner of the park. She crossed the road. She could only see the back of that house from the park. There was another road from which she'd be able to see the front.

An indulgence, certainly, but daydreaming was a new pastime for Jane. She needed some practice.

The real estate agent's sign on the front wall of the property was totally unexpected.

A sign in more ways than one?

Giving in to another impulse, Jane pulled her mobile phone from her briefcase and called the number on the sign. The enthusiastic agent asked if she could wait for ten minutes because he wasn't far away, the owners of the property were absent and he'd be only too delighted to show her around.

It was nearly dark by the time Jane had

finished the tour, assured the agent that, yes, she could well be interested, and set off, finally, for home. Her earlier weariness was gone. The combination of considering the job-sharing idea and then finding what looked like a perfect family home in the city was just too good to be true.

She'd known it was all falling into place before she'd even stepped through the front door of the house. When she'd seen that Christmas wreath hanging below the gold lion's-head knocker. The one that had artificial pohutukawa flowers instead of holly berries nestled amongst the green needles. A link to the cottage.

To Dylan.

She had to tell him.

Jane picked up the phone as soon as she was inside her apartment but then she checked her watch and put it down again. It was only 8.30 p.m. and it was Wednesday. Dylan would be working up at the little hospital, wouldn't he? She'd have to wait until after 11 p.m. to share the way their future seemed destined to fall into place.

But she couldn't wait. Jane paced the apartment. She should have some dinner but she wasn't the least bit hungry. She should be resting but, curiously, she'd never felt so wide-awake. So *alive*.

The idea came to her in a flash of what seemed no less than brilliance.

It was only a ninety-minute drive. Probably less in her little sports car.

She could be there, waiting at the cottage, when Dylan came home from work. She could tell him about the house. About being willing to cut her working hours. About how she wanted to change her life to be the best mother, and *wife*, that she could.

This wasn't about trying to earn Dylan's love. Or even to avoid the failure that was inevitable if she only made a half-hearted effort to make it work. It was about being true to herself. The real Jane. The Jane that had been left behind so many years ago in her grandmother's little house. It was about being prepared to love even if it didn't get returned in quite the way she might wish.

To avoid loving was to miss out on too much of what life had to offer. The best it had to offer, and she'd missed out on that for far, far too long.

Jane grabbed her wallet, snatched her car keys

from the hook near the door and ran down the stairs, oblivious to the smile on her face.

'You're a naughty boy, Dylan McKenzie.'

'It's a long time since anybody told me that, Enid.'

'You gave me two chocolate biscuits with my cocoa. I'll get fat.'

'What nonsense!' Dylan smiled at the tiny, frail old woman. 'You don't want to get too skinny, Enid. Men like enough to cuddle, you know.'

'Shame on you,' Enid scolded, but she was smiling broadly.

'It's getting late.' Dylan shifted his patient's pillows a little. 'Shall I tuck you up and turn out the light?'

'Yes, please, dear.'

The other elderly inpatients had been settled for some time and the observations Dylan needed to repeat on the teenager admitted with mild concussion didn't take long. His second shift at work was proving extremely quiet. Dylan was on his way to catch up with Marg and help her tidy the storeroom when Jennifer burst through the front door.

'Dylan! Are you busy?'

'No. It's very quiet.'

'We've got a call to an accident at the bottom of the hill. I'm just going to grab my trauma kit. Tell Marg where you're going and then meet me in the car park.'

'Sure.' Any threat of boredom in his new job evaporated and Dylan moved swiftly.

Minutes later they were speeding along the coast road in Jennifer's four-wheel-drive.

'It's been called in by one of our local police officers who was alerted by emergency services,' Jennifer told him. 'Apparently the driver made the call herself and said she was uninjured but he thinks she needs checking out.'

'What happened?'

'Sheep on the road. Driver swerved to avoid hitting it and hit the loose gravel instead. Car left the road and went over the side of the hill. Not much left by the sound of it. Low-slung sports cars are not made for off-road travel.'

'A sports car? At this time of night?' Sports

cars made Dylan think of Jane. Mind you, every-thing made him think of Jane these days.

'Stranger things have happened. It's how I met Drew again, in fact. At an accident scene on almost the same bit of road.' Jennifer smiled. 'He was driving a camper van, though, not a BMW.'

A BMW?

Dylan shook off the chill that ran down his spine. It couldn't be Jane.

Even if the driver was a woman?

His heart did a peculiar kind of flip. Thank God it wasn't Friday. He couldn't think of anything worse than to be heading for an accident scene knowing that Jane was the victim.

Jane sat on the side of the road.

Alone.

The policeman who had answered her call had parked his car uphill, with the lights flashing to warn oncoming traffic. He was now down the road towards the blind corner, putting out a sign and some bright plastic cones.

She hugged her knees tightly, but it wasn't enough to stop the shaking.

She wasn't hurt. Just…stunned.

Jane knew she hadn't been knocked out because she could remember everything in vivid detail. The shock of seeing something on the road in front of her as she rounded the bend. That awful moment when her wheels bit into loose shingle and lost traction. How time seemed to slow down as the car hurtled off the side of the road. The bang of hitting the fence post and the nasty smell of the dust released from the air bags exploding out from the steering-wheel and dashboard and even the top of her window.

Maybe she was bruised, because it did hurt a bit to take a deep breath. Tender areas where the safety belt had been across her chest and abdomen. And she was cold, despite the police officer's jacket over her shoulders. Exhaustion was creeping back and it was only now that Jane realised she hadn't eaten anything except a muffin since breakfast.

And now she wouldn't be able to surprise Dylan with her plans.

A single tear escaped and rolled down the side of her nose. And then another.

She wanted Dylan to be here. She wanted him to hold her and call her 'hinny' and tell her that everything was going to be all right.

A four-wheel-drive vehicle with a flashing light drove slowly past the cones and pulled up close to Jane. Two figures got out of the car and one looked familiar.

Big and strong and…wonderful.

Dylan!

Jane swallowed her tears and scrubbed at her face. She tried to stop the shaking so that she could make her lips co-operate enough to smile as Dylan walked towards her, a dark shadow with the glow of headlights behind him. But she couldn't manage the smile.

Dylan wasn't smiling, either.

'Are you hurt?'

'N-no.'

'Are you sure?'

'Y-yes. I'm f-fine.'

To her dismay, Dylan was looking anything but pleased to see her. She had never seen him look like this. So…*angry*. Why? Because she was here when she wasn't supposed to be? Because he didn't *want* her to be here? Tears gathered again and stung the backs of her eyes.

'How *could* you?' Dylan demanded. 'What the hell did you think you were doing?'

Jennifer was beside him now and she frowned at his tone. 'Are you sure you're not hurt, Jane?'

'I'm fine. Just…a bit shaken.'

Jennifer held out her hand. 'Do you think you can walk? We need to get you somewhere nice and warm and check you over properly.'

Jane got slowly to her feet with Jennifer's assistance. Dylan had turned away. He was staring at the mangled chassis of her car, wrapped around the fence post.

Jane choked back a sob. Why was he so angry with her?

Jennifer seemed to be wondering the same thing. 'It's all right,' she said to Jane reassuringly.

'*No.*' Dylan swung back to face them. 'It's not all right. Not at all! You could have been killed here, Jane.'

'I think she's quite well aware of that, Dylan.' Jennifer's tone was a warning.

One that Dylan ignored. He stepped forward and took hold of Jane's upper arms. The grip was tight.

'Sophie could have lost you,' he growled. 'She could have lost her mother! Did you stop to think about that before going for a joy ride in your fast wee car?'

'No.' Jane's voice was a croak. Something inside her was crumpling and she just wanted to curl up and cry. Dylan was angry because he was hurt. Somehow she had hurt this man she loved and it was the last thing she would have wanted to do.

How had it happened? Maybe she had bumped her head. It was hard to try and think clearly but something was taking shape. That was it. This was a terrible reminder of how Sophie had lost her birth parents. How Dylan had lost his brother.

'I'm sorry,' she said miserably.

'Dylan,' Jennifer said firmly. 'We really need to—'

'I should have been more responsible,' Jane carried on, as guilt took hold. 'I was tired and hadn't had anything to eat. I should have thought of Sophie. Of…of…'

'Of me!' Dylan roared. 'What about *me*?'

'*Dylan!*' Jennifer sounded truly shocked now.

Jane was losing track of what she wanted to say. 'What *about* you?'

Dylan seemed to be struggling to find words. His mouth opened and then closed. His face was creased in lines of…not anger…it was something deeper. Darker. Like despair.

Jane took a breath and found herself totally unable to let it go.

Maybe Jennifer did, too, because the night around them suddenly went very quiet. The whole world was holding its breath for a moment.

'*I* could have lost you,' Dylan whispered. 'Oh, God, hinny. I could have lost you and how could I live with that?'

'Oh-h-h…' Jennifer's soft exclamation was a sigh of comprehension. She backed away as Dylan lifted Jane into his arms and held her against her chest as easily as if she were a child.

Jane wound her arms around Dylan's neck and clung on to him as if her life depended on it.

Because it felt like it did.

'I love you, Dylan,' she said. 'I love you so much.'

Love.

It was all around her.

Jane could feel it in the way they took care of her up at the hospital on the hill, examining her bruises and taking X-rays of her ribs and neck.

'Just to be on the safe side,' Dylan insisted.

It was there in the way Marg and Ruby the cook fussed over her when Dylan took her to where Sophie was sleeping peacefully in the corner of the big old kitchens.

'You take your girls home,' Ruby instructed Dylan. 'And take good care of them.'

'Aye, I will.' Dylan nodded. 'Dinna fesh yourself aboot that.'

It was most definitely there when Sophie woke up and blinked sleepily at Jane, and then gave her the most achingly gorgeous smile she had ever seen. The way she held up her little arms.

'She wants her mother,' Dylan observed.

'That's me,' Jane whispered in wonder. 'That's

me!' She smiled at Dylan, with tears shining in her eyes. 'How good is that?'

Most of all, it was there in the way Dylan held her later. As though he never wanted to let her go. In the tender kisses he didn't seem to be able to stop himself pressing gently onto her hair. On her forehead. Even on the tip of her nose.

'I love that dimple,' he told her. 'I love *you*, Jane.'

'I love you, too.'

'Will you marry me?'

'Yes.' Jane laughed. 'I've already said yes. You've been to see the vicar already, haven't you?'

'Aye. But you were marrying me to be Sophie's mother. I want you to be marrying me for *me*.'

'I already was.'

'But I didn't know. You didn't tell me that, hinny.'

'That's because you were marrying me because I was Sophie's mother.'

'No.' Dylan's smile was slow in appearing but worth the wait. It was one of his best. 'She was just the ace up my sleeve. I knew Dr Jane Walters wouldn't want to marry a gypsy.'

'The real one does.' Jane was catching the

smile. She could feel it, seeping into her whole body. 'Are you still a gypsy, then?'

'No.' Dylan's gaze held Jane's. 'I've found what I was searching for. The place I want to be and the people I want to be with for the rest of my life. I found *you*, hinny. How good is that?'

And, finally, it was her lips that Dylan claimed with his kisses and it was a long time before Jane could speak again. When she did, it was with a smile that every cell in her being was contributing to.

'It's good,' she said. 'Very, *very* good.'

EPILOGUE

CHRISTMAS Eve at the bottom of the world was a summer's day as perfect as the ceremony that had just taken place in the tiny church on the top of a hill.

The new Mrs Jane McKenzie stood on the steps of the church, hand in hand with her husband. She wore a simple dress of white silk with a cross-over bodice that seemed to gather the full-length skirt so that it fell from one hip to ripple down to her feet, the small train pooling on the step above.

A single strand of her grandmother's pearls were around her neck and she carried a bunch of fragrant white Christmas lilies. Her hair was loose, the way Dylan loved it most, but a section had been pulled back into a high clasp and woven into the twisted tresses were the small, crimson flowers of the pohutukawa.

Dylan wore a single red bloom of the New Zealand Christmas tree in the lapel of his black jacket and the colour was a match for the line in the McKenzie tartan of the kilt he wore.

'It's the old McKenzie tartan,' he'd explained. 'The green is for the forests and fields. The blue for the sky and the sea. White is for purity and the red for blood and bold fighters.'

It was perfect.

The green was all around them in the trees and hills. Her dress was white because this was her first wedding and it would be the only one because she was with the man she loved enough to spend the rest of her life with. The blue of the sea below was a reflection of the cloudless summer sky. Beautiful, but not nearly as dark or compelling as the blue of Dylan's eyes.

The final, haunting notes of 'Highland Wedding' came from where Dylan's father, Angus, was playing his bagpipes, at the point where the velvet lawn created the edge of the hilltop.

Dylan bent to kiss his bride and provide the

photograph that Angus would put in pride of place on the mantelpiece of the new home he already loved. Angus was a real McKenzie. A bold fighter whose fierce love for his son and his granddaughter made him more than ready to embark on a new life in a new country. A love that already included his new daughter-in-law.

Still hand in hand, the bride and groom moved down the steps to join Angus as the select group of wellwishers emerged from the church. They both looked down at the village below for a moment and Jane smiled. Down there, hidden in the village, was the tiny patch of this earth that had become—more than it had ever been—her touchstone. Inside the cottage there were white vases filled with flowers from the pohutukawa tree, and in front of the fireplace was a slightly lopsided branch of spruce tree that had a gold star on the top.

Their honeymoon would be celebrating Christmas in the cottage. A time for family and gifts and contentment. A perfect way to start a new life together. A place where contentment didn't need to be rationed any more because when she had to return to 'reality', the most important parts of that contentment would be coming with her.

Her husband.

And her daughter.

As if on cue, a plump woman came forward from the group now gathered at the bottom of the church steps. Ruby carried a bassinette she had decorated with white satin that had bows of ribbon in McKenzie tartan. Marg had made Sophie's dress in record time. A soft, white muslin dress with a smocked top and tiny red flowers embroidered into the smocking.

Jane lifted her daughter from the bassinette and held her within the circle of Dylan's arm as the final moment of this ceremony began. The tribute they had chosen as their way of including Izzy and Josh in this day.

Jennifer and Drew's children came forward with a white hexagonal box which they placed on the grass in front of the newlyweds before removing the lid. Inside were dozens of monarch butterflies to be released as a symbol of love and new life. And as a way to remember the spirits of loved ones that couldn't be there.

'Izzy adored butterflies,' Jane had explained to Dylan. 'They will always remind me of her.'

One by one, the butterflies climbed to the top of the box and took flight in glorious bursts of orange and black. More and more emerged. Some flew away and some hovered. One landed in Jane's hair to explore the flowers.

Sophie's eyes grew round with wonder and her mouth curved into the grin that Jane loved so much. She reached up with both hands towards the butterflies and Jane tilted her head as she laughed, hoping to catch Dylan's gaze and share this joy.

And this would be *her* favourite photograph.

Butterflies filling the air like jewels. The smile on their baby's face. The intensity of the love being communicated between the bride and groom.

And…oh, yes…the way that puff of breeze was lifting the corner of Dylan's kilt so tantalisingly…

MEDICAL™

Large Print

Titles for the next three months...

June

SNOWBOUND: MIRACLE MARRIAGE	Sarah Morgan
CHRISTMAS EVE: DOORSTEP DELIVERY	Sarah Morgan
HOT-SHOT DOC, CHRISTMAS BRIDE	Joanna Neil
CHRISTMAS AT RIVERCUT MANOR	Gill Sanderson
FALLING FOR THE PLAYBOY MILLIONAIRE	Kate Hardy
THE SURGEON'S NEW-YEAR WEDDING WISH	Laura Iding

July

POSH DOC, SOCIETY WEDDING	Joanna Neil
THE DOCTOR'S REBEL KNIGHT	Melanie Milburne
A MOTHER FOR THE ITALIAN'S TWINS	Margaret McDonagh
THEIR BABY SURPRISE	Jennifer Taylor
NEW BOSS, NEW-YEAR BRIDE	Lucy Clark
GREEK DOCTOR CLAIMS HIS BRIDE	Margaret Barker

August

EMERGENCY: PARENTS NEEDED	Jessica Matthews
A BABY TO CARE FOR	Lucy Clark
PLAYBOY SURGEON, TOP-NOTCH DAD	Janice Lynn
ONE SUMMER IN SANTA FE	Molly Evans
ONE TINY MIRACLE...	Carol Marinelli
MIDWIFE IN A MILLION	Fiona McArthur

MILLS & BOON®